RED DIRT BLUES

DAVID K WILSON

Cover design by Caroline Johnson

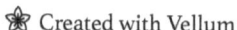 Created with Vellum

1

The beautiful woman with long, jet black hair quietly rifled through the files stuffed in the bottom drawer of the mahogany desk, trying not to rouse the suspicions of the Russian mobster tied to the bed in the other room.

"Where are you, kitten?" the Russian sing-songed.

"Just one more minute, sexy," the woman purred back in Russian.

Anton Petrov, the bound mobster in the other room, relaxed back in his bed as best as one can while being tied spread-eagle. As he lay in wait, he began to marvel in gratitude at how his entire night had changed just because he decided to have one more drink. One of Anton's many duties was managing Kozel's, a swank nightclub located on the edge of Moscow City and next door to Anton's high-rise apartment building. It was a place where Russian dignitaries, high-powered businessmen, and visiting celebrities often gathered. While he had a brutal reputation, Anton still lived under the shadow of his brother, the notorious crime boss Viktor Petrov. Kozel's was the place where Anton could be king. He often held court at his VIP booth, separated from the masses by red velvet ropes and two giant bodyguards, and positioned on a riser so he could look down on his kingdom. The raised platform also made sure everyone in the bar was able to see the short hairy man in a snakeskin jacket.

He had nearly left earlier but was cajoled into one more drink by a jovial group of visiting Polish businessmen who had dealings with Anton's brother. He had been instructed to keep the men entertained and Anton had seen to it that their vodka glasses were never empty. The decision to have one more drink with them was the best decision he had ever made. Because that's when he saw *her*. She was sitting at the bar alone and, just as importantly, gazing directly at him. Even though he was constantly surrounded by Russian models, the exotic beauty of this woman immediately caught his attention. She had full lips, high cheekbones and beautiful, seductive eyes that captured his attention and immediately fueled his desire. When their gaze locked, she smiled flirtatiously. Encouraged, Anton immediately forgot about the Polish businessmen. He called a waiter over and ordered a glass of champagne for the woman, with instructions to also invite her to his table. Even though he was no prize catch, he had money. And power. And that was enough for many of the young ladies that frequented the bar. In fact, so many women had been seduced by his money and power (or more than willing to accept his money for a few hours of their time), that he had fooled himself into believing they actually found him attractive.

He watched the woman accept the glass of champagne and then nod in understanding as the waiter extended the invitation to join the bar's owner. She looked at Anton, winked at him, then stood to walk over. He was now able to see more of her and unconsciously let out a loud gasp in appreciation. Her deep-cut, red evening gown showed off her svelte, athletic body. A slit cut all the way up to her right hip, revealing every inch of her perfectly-toned leg...and a little bit more. She walked with confidence but remained approachable. By the time she reached the table, Anton was barely able to muster a greeting.

Her seductive charms quickly unarmed him and they began their flirtatious dance. Her name was Khristina and she was visiting from Prague. She was friendly and flirty. Incredibly sexual but not intimidating. And very open to Anton's clumsy advances. In less than an hour, they had moved their dance to his penthouse apartment. And before he knew it, she had undressed him to his underwear, blindfolded him and bound him to the bed, promising him unimaginable pleasure.

She doesn't know how good my imagination is, he thought to himself.

She had excused herself to prepare something special and he now waited with eager anticipation.

However, Khristina clearly had other things on her mind as she looked around the giant penthouse living room.

2

From the sleek, modern furniture to the original artwork, the place reeked of money. And was clearly put together by an interior decorator, not the short, round slob of a man in the next room. The floor-to-ceiling windows looked out over the spectacular skyline of Moscow City. Postmodern glass buildings outlined in brilliant blue and red lights jutted high into the night sky, looking like a breathtaking metropolis of the future. But she wasn't paying attention to the view. She was looking at the large, built-in bookshelf behind the desk. Binders, notepads and books were carelessly stacked on each shelf so precariously that removing any item would send the entire structure crumbling to the floor. It was the only area of the living room that wasn't perfectly staged so Jade knew it was the area used the most and where she would most likely find what she was looking for.

Catching a glimpse of her reflection in one of the many glass sculptures in the room, she couldn't help but smile in appreciation of how she looked. She made a stunning Russian supermodel. Certainly good enough to attract the attention of

Antov Petrov, the younger brother of the most notorious Russian crime boss in Moscow.

Antov's well-known love for beautiful women and his oversized ego were his Achilles' Heel and she was able to take advantage of them with little effort. It took less than an hour of pretending to be interested in his boring stories and laughing at his obnoxious jokes, before he invited her up to his penthouse apartment.

Promising a night he'd never forget (and truly meaning it), she had bound him spread-eagle to his four-post, king-size bed then covered his eyes with a necktie.

With Antov happily restrained, she was able to search his apartment with ease, stoking his fire with an occasional "I'm nearly ready!" But she was running out of places to look.

ANTON PLAYFULLY STRUGGLED with the ties that bound him, counting his blessing and anticipating the night in front of him. Khristina was not only more beautiful than any Russian woman he had ever seen, but she actually seemed interested in him. When he had first put his hand on her bare thigh, she didn't flinch. And when she pushed his roaming hand away, she promised she'd let him touch her everywhere before the night was through.

What in the world could she be doing? he wondered. *Was she putting on a sexy costume? Her handbag wasn't big enough to hold anything too elaborate. Or was she preparing some kind of makeshift sex toy? Whatever it was, he felt certain it would be worth the wait.*

"I promise it will be worth the wait, my tiger," Khristina purred from the other room, repeating his thoughts.

Anton settled back in the bed and resigned himself to waiting patiently. It was what he did best. Being the younger brother of Viktor Petrov, he had grown used to waiting. Waiting for permission. Waiting for orders. Waiting for the all-clear. There had been a time when he was feared and respected. His violent temper was almost legendary. But when his brother took charge he had learned to keep it in check. Now his temper could have broader implications. Attacking the wrong man at the wrong time could jeopardize business deals and criminal alliances. So now he played host to drunk businessmen and waited for his brother's orders.

But for all the waiting, he never complained. It was a life that had afforded him many luxuries. Like his penthouse apartment. And the ability to spend ludicrous amounts of money on women in order to lure them back to the penthouse apartment. Still, even though he was a Vor—the Russian equivalent of a "made man" in the Sicilian mafia—he knew everyone thought of him as a joke. He was the mladshiy brat. The little brother. But Viktor protected him. Not just because they were siblings. It was because of Anton's loyalty. The Russian Bratva was filled with backstabbers and liars. Anton knew Viktor was the only person he could truly trust and that made him more valuable than anything else.

The sound of glass shattering startled Anton.

"What was that?" Anton yelled out.

His instinct was to check on the sound and he struggled with the bindings a little harder. They were more secure than he had originally thought.

"Just a champagne glass. I'll clean it up."

"Clean it later. I am growing restless."

"You're not being a bad boy, are you?" Khristina teased.

He could tell she had walked into the bedroom and was instantly reminded of why he was restrained. It was enough to lull him back into a state of happy and helpless lust.

"I'm just getting out a few toys for us," she explained in a very sultry voice.

"If you need toys, I have plenty," he said. "In the drawer by the bed. And the top shelf in the closet. Also, the top drawer of the dresser by the window."

"Oh, I have something special in mind," Khristina replied. "I promise you won't be disappointed."

She grabbed Anton's discarded shirt from the pile of clothes on the floor and walked back into the office, clearly disgusted by her bound comrade. She had cut herself on the broken glass and used the shirt to wipe the blood from the gash on the palm of her hand. Finding a pair of scissors, she quietly cut off a portion of one of the sleeves and created a makeshift bandage that she wrapped around her hand before returning to the bookshelf and removing a blue binder.

"Come on. Where are you hiding it?" she muttered under her breath...in perfect English.

3

Anton continued to wait patiently, a million dirty thoughts dancing in his head like X-rated sugar plum fairies. Then he heard the clack of high heels walk into the room and he caught his breath in anticipation.

"Anton, we have a bit of a problem," Khristina said matter-of-factly.

Anton was confused. For one, she didn't sound very sexy at all. But more importantly, she wasn't speaking Russian. In fact, it seemed to be perfect English. But the confusion soon turned into arousal and a dirty grin spread across his face.

"Ohhh. Role play," he said in Russian before clearing his voice and speaking broken English in his heavy Russian accent. "You will not get what you look for, American scum."

He quickly broke character to clarify the situation.

"I'm assuming you're supposed to be an American spy or something?" he asked in Russian.

He could feel Khristina sit down on the bed next to him, but instead of a light, teasing touch, she yanked the tie that had been doubling as a blindfold off of his face. Anton squinted to focus. He was confused. Khristina wasn't dressed as a sexy spy. In fact, she was still wearing the same dress she had on earlier.

"Where is it, Anton?" she asked again in English.

He was distracted by the bandage on Jade's hand.

"Is that my shirt?"

She ignored him.

"The goat, Anton."

He returned his focus to the task at hand. If she was willing to continue the role play, he was game. He answered her in his Russian-accented English.

"Right between my legs, you capitalist swine."

Khristina shook her head.

"No," she said impatiently. "Where's the goat?"

More confused than ever, Anton broke character again.

"I feel like I need to know the scene to do this properly," he said. "Maybe we just go over the basic scenario then I promise not to interrupt anymore."

"I need the goat, Anton."

Anton nodded, pretending to understand and resuming his character.

"Yes. And I have goat that you cannot have. So, ha-HA!"

Khristina, standing over Anton, smiled.

"Tell me where the goat is," she demanded.

"You will never get goat. You must torture first. Possibly with what you find in drawer," he said, motioning to the drawer of his nightstand.

Khristina shook her head and pulled a knife out from behind her back.

"I don't think you're taking me seriously, Anton."

Upon seeing the knife, Anton broke character yet again.

"I think we may need a safe word."

Khristina traced the tip of the knife down his abdomen to the hem of his boxers.

Anton was beginning to get scared. He pulled on his restrains.

"Khristina?"

"I prefer Jade," she said.

Anton's eyes grew wide with fear at the sound of the name. He began to wrestle against the restraints.

"Now we can do this the easy way," the woman formerly known as Khristina said as she guided the blade further down between his legs.

"Or the hard way."

Anton could barely breath. He could feel the sweat dripping off his forehead.

"I am so confused and so turned on right now."

Jade straddled him and put the knife to his throat.

"We're not playing a game, asshole," she said. "Your brother took something that didn't belong to him and I want it back. Now."

Anton felt the sharp tip of the knife pressing against his skin. He saw the cold fury in Jades's eyes. Finally, reality started to sink in and his fear started to burn into a defiant anger.

"I don't know what you're talking about," he said.

"You see? That's a problem," Jade said. "Because I don't believe you. So just tell me where it is and I'll be quietly on my way."

Anton quickly glanced at his dresser without thinking then glared at his captor.

"I will tell you nothing," he growled.

Jade smirked. "You just did."

She crawled off of Anton and started going through the drawers of the dresser, tossing out clothes and a myriad of odd sex toys. As she looked, Anton began to twist the bedpost where his right hand was tied. After being left spread-eagle too many times by greedy prostitutes, Anton had made the four posts of his bed removable. With just a few twists, they could easily be removed from the bed so he could free himself. With Jade preoccupied by the dresser, he was able to quietly disassemble the right post. As she looked for hidden compartments, he slowly reached to his nightstand and opened the drawer, grabbing a pistol.

But before he could lift the gun out of the drawer, he felt a sharp pain. He looked down in shock to see the knife Jade had just hurled into his chest.

4

Thirty minutes later, a jet black Jaguar F-Type sped down the M-11, one of Russia's main highways. Maneuvering between other cars at a high speed, Jade drove calmly and in complete control. She dialed a number on her cell phone and it rang through the car's speakers.

"You're early," a man said on the other end.

It was Donovan Fontaine. The wealthy French baron who had hired Jade. She had worked for him almost exclusively the last several years. Even though he had a reputation as a ruthless pirate who had no qualms getting rid of anything - or anyone - that stood in his way, his assignments were normally cut and dry and her percentage was more generous than most others.

"He didn't have it," Jade replied.

"Are you sure?"

"It already shipped," Jade said coldly.

"How do you know?"

"He gave me the shipping ledger."

"He gave it to you?"

"In so many words."

"Please tell me you didn't kill him," Donovan said through gritted teeth.

"I had no choice. You know how I work, Donovan. You've never complained before."

"Now his brother is going to get involved," Donovan chastised. "I don't need the Russian mob involved in this."

Jade removed the long black wig and tousled her short, black hair.

"Then you shouldn't have sent me into the belly of the beast," Jade replied.

"He's going to retaliate. And it's going to come down on you before it does on me."

"I can handle Viktor Petrov," Jade assured him.

"Did you at least find out where it is now?" Donovan asked with a sigh.

"Texas," Jade answered. "Red Dirt, Texas."

5

The stack of plastic FOR SALE signs hit the cluttered counter with a crash that was louder than Randy Philpot had intended. He immediately apologized, but the ninety-year-old cashier barely even looked up from her paperback.

"Hey, Randy," Eunice Carter said in a monotone Texas twang.

"Hey, Miss Carter," Randy replied. "You doing alright?"

"I woke up today so I can't rightly complain," the old woman said as she sat her book down to ring up the sale.

Randy nodded with a slight smile. As long as Randy could remember, Miss Carter had been the old woman that worked the cash register at the hardware store. In his thirty-three years, he couldn't recall ever seeing her come out from behind the counter. Or even get up from her chair. For all he knew, she didn't have any legs.

Randy had grown up in Red Dirt and knew everyone in town. Of course, with a population of only 65 people, that wasn't too hard to do. What was impressive was that not everyone in town knew Randy. He had a way of just blending in. A trick made easier by having to live in the shadow of his recently-deceased older brother and his domineering mother. A lanky man with kind eyes and a gentle smile, Randy was the reliable guy who would do what you asked without making a fuss. The kind of guy that you didn't so much count on, but simply take for granted. But even though Randy blended in easily, he never felt like he fit in.

"How are you doing, given the state of things?" Miss Carter asked.

Randy absent-mindedly scratched his head, unwittingly creating a cowlick in his blonde hair.

"Just keeping busy," he replied, not really wanting to talk about the things in question. "In fact, I was fixing to head to the shop so..."

"How's your mama holding up?" Miss Carter asked again, ignoring his hint.

"Oh, you know Mama," Randy answered with a shrug.

Miss Carter nodded as she slowly rang up the FOR SALE signs.

"She's a tough one," she said. "Still, I know Clyde was her favorite. No offense."

Randy should have been stunned by Miss Carter's bluntness, but he had grown used to it. And he knew it was true. He just nodded and turned his attention to a man even older than the cashier who was shuffling up to the counter. The name POOTER was embroidered on the upper left side of his red work vest.

"Hey, Mr. Carter," Randy said.

Pooter looked at the stack of FOR SALE signs.

"You ain't moving, are you?" he asked, talking loud enough so he could hear his own voice.

"Oh, no," Randy answered. "These are for the shop."

"The Lazy Goat?" Miss Carter asked.

"Yes, ma'am," Randy answered.

"Damn shame," Pooter yelled. "That store's a town landmark."

Randy shrugged.

"Not enough customers," he explained. "I honestly don't know how Clyde stayed in business as long as he did."

He turned his attention back to Miss Carter, who was still ringing up the third sign.

"Give me a hand over here, Randy," Pooter yelled.

"I really need to get going," he answered.

Pooter shuffled over to a wheelbarrow near one of the aisles of the hardware store. He was either ignoring Randy or just hadn't heard him.

"I need you to put these bags on that shelf," Pooter yelled.

Randy looked down at the bags in the wheelbarrow. They were all labeled FRESH MANURE. Realizing it was going to be awhile before Miss Carter was finished ringing up his items, he sighed.

"Which shelf?"

With Pooter's direction, Randy hoisted each 50-pound bag up on the empty metal shelf with a heavy groan. Randy was skinny, but not puny. Still, lifting the bags up to the waist-high shelf took an effort. As he sat the last bag down with a thud, he watched helplessly as some of the contents leaked out on his blue jeans. He winced at the smell but didn't say a thing.

"Good job," Pooter said. "Just one more wheelbarrow."

6

_____

By the time Randy finished his forced volunteer shift at the hardware store, it was late afternoon. His old Ford pick-up chugged down the two-lane road, through the deep piney woods of northeast Texas toward Red Dirt. Occasionally, he would drive past a pasture where a handful of cattle would be grazing, or a small, run-down home littered with colorful plastic children's toys. The trees grew sparce as he passed a small, single-pump gas station and neared the center of Red Dirt, marked with a four-way intersection with two stop signs. The local Baptist Church was positioned on the left corner of the intersection. Across the street to his right was a small grocery store. In front of him, on the left, was the red and white PERTY'S sign, marking the town's one and only restaurant. And finally, across the street on the right, was a modest hand-painted sign that read THE LAZY GOAT.

Randy pulled into the empty dirt parking lot of The Lazy Goat, kicking up a cloud of red dust as he pulled up to the spot closest to the entrance.

With the engine still running so he could keep taking advantage of the truck's AC, Randy opened a water bottle and rummaged through the glove apartment for a napkin. Unfortunately, what he found was a tattered picture of Shelley Lansing, his ex-girlfriend. His heart immediately took a nose dive. Randy paused to stare at the photo of the blonde beauty with big blue eyes.

HE HAD THOUGHT he had found his one and only. He'd known Shelley since high school, but it wasn't until after he had returned from Austin that the relationship turned romantic. It wasn't long until they were both madly in love and talking about building a life together. Shelley's father had offered Randy a job at his pipe fitting factory. They were gonna get married, raise some little ones and live the Red Dirt dream. And then, out of the blue, it all came crashing down. Randy still wasn't sure what happened.

Letting out a loud sigh, he placed the photo back in the glove compartment, vowing to himself that he would get rid of it. Soon. But before he could procrastinate even more, a loud knock on the truck window caught him off guard. He jerked in surprise, spilling water all over his shirt, and turned to see a woman standing outside of his truck.

The pain and heartache quickly scurried back to the corners of his mind where they would wait to ambush him another day. He didn't recognize the woman, which was a rare thing in Red Dirt. She was definitely from out of town. Probably out of state. While her Farrah Fawcett blonde hair and tight jeans were all Texas, there was something about her deep blue eyes that gave her away as a visitor. He could always tell by their eyes. He couldn't put his finger on what it was, but he'd never been wrong yet.

"You okay in there?" she asked with a thick Texas accent.

Randy nodded and rolled his window down, attempting to wipe his shirt dry with the other hand.

"Are y'all open?" she asked.

Randy looked around for another car, but the parking lot was empty.

Where did she even come from? he wondered.

"Sorry, ma'am. We're closed."

"You fixin' to open?" she asked.

"No," Randy explained. "We're closed closed. As in out of business closed."

The woman pouted.

"But I came so far!" she said. "My cousin Shelby from Beaumont told me all about this place and I got in the car and drove all day. I love goats! I've been collecting goats since I was a little girl. Please?"

Randy smiled. It never ceased to amaze him that there were people interested in his brother's store. But then again, not many were, which was why he was shutting it down.

"The owner passed away," Randy explained.

She gasped.

"Clyde Philpot is dead?" she asked.

"You knew him?"

"I spoke to him on the phone not that long ago," She said. "When did he die?"

"Two days ago."

"Dear Lord. It was probably three or four days ago I talked to him," she said. "He was gonna set aside a little figurine for me."

Randy told her that he didn't remember seeing anything set aside, but the woman pleaded for him to look one last time. It didn't take much for Randy to agree. The pangs of loneliness he had stirred up when he saw Shelley's picture jumped at the chance to spend a few more minutes with someone. Especially a gorgeous woman. It was just the sort of distraction he needed.

Randy got out of his truck and noticed the woman glancing at his wet shirt and stained pants.

"I've had a rough day," he explained.

She flashed a big "I'm so sorry" smile and Randy reciprocated with a shy nod. As he walked to the storefront door, fumbling with a mass of keys on a large key ring, the woman walked behind him, absentmindedly rubbing the scratch on her left palm.

7

She followed Randy into the large showroom and stopped in surprise at what laid before her. There were probably eight aisles of white shelves, each standing about five feet high and filled with an incredible assortment of porcelain goat figurines.

Some were large, about the size of a small chihuahua. Others were tiny - barely the size of a dime. There were natural-looking goats and goats dressed in clothes. Solid white goats. Colorful goats. If a goat was made out of porcelain or glass, it was probably on one of the shelves.

"Oh my Lord," she muttered.

"Yeah," Randy agreed.

"People really buy all of these?" she asked.

"Apparently not all of 'em," Randy said. "I'm sorry. Where are my manners? I'm Randy Philpot. Clyde's brother"

"His brother?" she asked. "I'm so sorry. Can I ask what happened? He seemed just fine when I talked to him."

Randy shook his head. "Idiot got shit-faced drunk and decided to take a whiz on an electrical transformer."

They both winced at the thought of it.

"At least it was quick," Randy said with a shrug.

He walked behind the counter. "Now you said he set something aside for you?"

As Randy looked under the counter and on the shelves behind the register, the woman wandered the aisles, mesmerized by all the goat figures.

"You know what it is?" Randy asked.

"It came from Russia," she replied.

"Unfortunately, a lot of his stuff did," Randy answered. "So much for 'Made in the U.S. of A.'"

"It was a little white goat figurine," she said, looking around at the rows and rows of little white goat figurines. "Had a red dot on the base."

Randy told her he'd check the back and disappeared down a side door. The woman began to wander the shelves, turning over each figurine in search for a red dot.

A loud KNOCK on the front door startled her and she immediately ducked behind the shelves. She peered over the top to see a man in a cowboy hat and light brown uniform. The bright Texas sun glinted off a gold badge on his chest.

8

V ladimar Reznikov sat nervously on the edge of the couch, his foot tapping involuntarily. He had been summoned to the non-descript office with instructions to not be late and to sit down and wait...something he had now been doing for forty-five minutes. The wait was clearly meant as a power move to put him on edge and it was definitely working.

Up until this morning, Vlad had been Anton Petrov's bodyguard. He was the one who found the body, still restrained on the bed in boxers and socks but with a large knife wound in his chest and a pool of blood underneath him. To avoid a criminal investigation, the body had been discreetly disposed of and the murder scene had been cleaned thoroughly. Before he could breathe a sigh of relief, Vlad received the phone call that Viktor Petrov himself wanted to meet with him.

He jumped at the sound of the door opening and stood at the sight of the crime boss. He bowed his head respectfully as Viktor walked in with a calm confidence that only comes from complete control. And the reassurance of knowing you have two huge bodyguards flanking you on either side.

Without expression, Viktor Petrov nodded at Vlad, motioning for him to sit back down. Tall, fit and dignified, Viktor was in many ways the exact opposite of his brother Anton. He adjusted the dark purple tie and unbuttoned the breast of his tailored suit jacket before sitting in a leather chair opposite Vlad.

The room was deadly quiet and Viktor languished in it, studying the nervous man sitting across from him. Not sure what he should do, Vlad looked at the ground, then at Viktor than at the two giant men standing behind Viktor.

Known infamously as the Koslov Twins, they served as Viktor's bodyguards and personal enforcers. Peter Koslov was tall and muscular and, based on his tailored suit and tie, clearly shared the same sense of fashionable pride as his boss. Flanking Viktor's other side was Leo Koslov, who looked identical to his brother in all but two very noticeable ways. While he did wear a tailored suit, he did not wear a tie, his open collar revealing the other difference: a snake tattoo that seemed to climb up his neck and flick its tongue at his earlobe.

The silence was so thick that Vlad jumped when Viktor finally spoke.

"So you were the one who found my brother?" Viktor asked in Russian.

Vlad nodded, chains of sweat pouring from his forehead. He told Viktor about the crime scene. The knife wound. How they had followed protocol precisely and disposed of the body. As he spoke, he choked up.

"Anton was a good man," Vlad said, "He was like a brother to me."

The words fell out of his mouth before he could stop them and Vlad looked up at the dead man's actual brother sitting across from him. But Viktor's expression had not changed. It was still as cold and expressionless as it had been when he first walked in the room.

"Where were you when it happened?" Viktor asked. "When you were supposed to be guarding him?"

Viktor watched as Vlad began to hyperventilate, assessing the man's every move, looking for clues of any kind. Finally, Vlad composed himself enough to speak.

"I was right outside of the door," Vlad said. "He didn't want me to come in while he was…"

"While he was what?"

"The woman," Vlad said. "He had a woman in his room earlier."

Viktor's jaw clenched at the mention of the woman. He had Vlad walk through the events of the evening. When Anton and the woman had met. When they had entered the apartment. When she had left. What she had looked like.

"Had anything else in the apartment been touched? What about his desk?"

Vlad shrugged.

"It was covered in files and notebooks, but it was always like that."

Without taking his eyes off of Vlad, Viktor spoke to the two men behind him.

"I need all the security footage from the building. Anything with this woman he had been with. What was the name you said?"

"Khristina," Vlad answered.

Viktor smirked and stood, buttoning his suit jacket again.

"That's not her real name," he said to Vlad.

As he walked out the door, he spoke back to his two henchmen.

"Kill him."

9

I n a small beige office tucked along the wall of FBI headquarters in Washington, D.C., Special Agent Dean Bennett slid a thick manila folder across a desk.

His boss, Deputy Assistant Director Rudy Strickland, opened the folder with a sigh and looked at the blurred picture of a woman. He leafed through the huge stack of contents, which included several reports, crime files and photos.

"This is all you've got?" he asked sarcastically.

"I've been tracking her for years," Dean replied.

Strickland half-heartedly rifled through the papers.

"These are all the crimes you THINK she committed," he said. "What do you actually have on her? Stats? Background? A decent profile?"

"She doesn't leave much of a paper trail," Dean replied enthusiastically. "But I know there's something."

Dean was in his mid-fifties but most everybody assumed he was older. With a perpetually receding hairline and hangdog face, he had always looked older than his actual age. Wearing a short-sleeved white dress shirt and conservative black tie, he looked more like an accountant than an FBI agent, which was probably appropriate, considering he worked in the bureau's Information Management Division.

"The only name we know is Jade," Dean continued. "I'm assuming that's an alias."

Dean reached across the desk and pulled out a series of photos. They were surveillance photos taken of the windows of Anton's apartment from another building. Telephoto images had zoomed in through the windows into Anton's bedroom and, while they were grainy and hard to see, there was clearly a body on a bed.

"We believe this was her latest victim," Dean continued. "Anton Petrov, the younger brother of Viktor Petrov."

He pulled another photo forward. This one was of a man dressed in a fashionable suit and designer sunglasses. He had a pronounced square jaw and a visible scar across his cheek.

"He's the Pakhan of the Petrov crime family," Strickland said.

Dean nodded. "The big cheese himself."

"So why hit his brother?" Strickland asked.

"Not sure. A warning? Retaliation?" Dean explained, happy to take the bait. "What we do know is Viktor was very protective of his little brother and this murder will no doubt incite a nasty retaliation. His murder makes no sense unless–"

"Unless it wasn't a hit," Strickland interrupted.

"I'm thinking it was a retrieval job gone bad," Dean said. "Security cameras caught Jade leaving the building."

"You mean, a person you SUSPECT is Jade," the director corrected. "Where's the body? What do the Moscow police say?"

Dean sighed.

"There is no body. They clearly disposed of it and no police report was filed. If it wasn't for these surveillance photos..."

"That really show nothing," the director interrupted.

Dean nodded but continued anyway.

"The Petrov clan are known traffickers. Jewelry. Arms. Drugs. Intelligence. Maybe she was looking for something."

"This mess is all happening in Russia, right?" Strickland said, skimming over the report. "This is their problem."

"The police aren't investigating," Dean replied. "You know how it goes. Pockets are lined. People look away. But interest isn't with the Petrovs. It's with Jade. I'm tracking some intel that tells me she may be heading to America and it could be our best shot at finally catching her."

Strickland studied the blurred photo of the woman again. He looked through the files at blurred photos of other women. They all wore sunglasses and sported different color hair. They could be anyone in a variety of disguises. Or different people altogether.

"This is seriously all you've got?" he asked.

"Sir, I've been following her work for years," Dean enthused. "She's a skilled thief and a cold-blooded killer. I've been able to track over 30 heists in the past five years' worth over 2 billion dollars. And the body count is impressive. Twenty-two, that we know of. She's one of the best. And she's been working under the radar for a decade."

"Impressive?" Strickland asked. "You sound like the president of her fan club."

He leaned back in his chair with a groan. This wasn't the first time Dean had come to him with a paper-thin theory. Granted, that was part of his job. As an analyst in the Intelligence Division of the FBI, Dean's responsibilities included sifting through data and other intelligence to spot trends or abnormalities.

"No discerning characteristics. The doorman said she was tall, had dark hair and glasses. Along with hundreds of other women in Moscow that night. She could be anyone. And anywhere," Strickland said.

"But if we can find out what she was looking for, we may be

able to get ahead of her," Dean protested. "This may be our only shot."

"IF she was looking for something and IF she hasn't already found it, and IF we can figure out what it is, then we MAY be able to track her to it," Strickland summarized. "Am I getting this right?"

"It's the best shot we've ever had," Dean answered, the wind clearly leaving his sails.

"At least give me a chance to dig a little deeper," Dean said. "See if I can find anything."

Strickland smiled at Dean's energy. He stood, signaling the meeting was over. Dean stood as well, optimistically waiting for his boss's answer.

"Sorry, Dean," Strickland said. "But I really need you to concentrate on other things right now."

Dean nodded. He half-expected the answer.

Strickland walked around his desk and opened the door to see Dean out. Dean could almost feel his pity. It was something he had grown used to. At least pity was somewhat sympathetic. It was better than the sarcasm and derision that was usually thrown at him. Dean had been with the Bureau for over twenty years and had never really fit in with the other agents.

As he walked back to his cubicle, he looked down at the blurred photo of Jade. He had been following her profile for years and had come to know her as well as anyone could. He felt like if he could get even just a small lead, he could track her down. If standard procedure wasn't going to work, then he'd have to try a different route.

The man with the badge knocked on the door again and Randy came running out from the backroom.

"Hold your horses, Sheriff," he said as he ran to the front door and unlocked it.

Sheriff McKinley stepped inside. A grizzled, barrel-chested man in his fifties with a sour expression on his bearded face.

"Hey, Randy," McKinley said. "I saw your truck and just wanted to check on you and your mama."

He looked at the woman who was hidden behind the shelves as she browsed through the goat figurines.

"You got company?" McKinley asked.

"Just a customer," he said.

"I thought you were closing down," the sheriff prodded.

He looked at the woman, who seemed to be purposefully staying out of sight, and then back to Randy, putting a mystery together and then solving it with a big grin.

"I didn't interrupt anything, did I?" he asked with a wink.

"What? No!" Randy protested.

The sheriff looked back toward the woman, who was now standing motionless behind the shelves. He leaned in to Randy.

"Then why is she hiding back there?" he whispered. "No pants on or something?"

Before Randy could protest, she walked around from behind the shelf with a big smile.

"Oh, Randy, why fight it?" she said. "He's clearly on to us."

Randy was confused as this woman he had just met walked toward him. But she spoke before he could say anything.

"I'm Jen," she said, extending her hand to the sheriff. "Jen Brown."

"Nice to meet you, Jen," the sheriff replied as he shook her hand. "Sorry if I interrupted anything here."

"Just trying to be discreet," Jen said with a wink. "Randy wants to keep things on the down-low because of the funeral and all."

Randy laughed nervously, too confused to say anything.

"I get that," the sheriff laughed. "Where you from, Jen Brown?"

"Dallas," she answered.

"Dallas, huh? Well, don't go corrupting our boy here with big city thoughts."

McKinley winked at Jen and patted a stunned-in-place Randy on the shoulder.

"Randy, I'm real sorry about your brother," he said, turning serious on a dime. "I know he and I had our differences, but he was a good man."

Randy felt relieved he finally understood what someone was saying and latched on to it.

"I appreciate you saying so, Sheriff. But we both know that ain't true," he said. "Hell, you know it better than anyone."

The sheriff smiled and nodded.

"Well, you give your mama my condolences just the same," he said before turning to Jen. "And it was nice meeting you, ma'am."

"Same here, Sheriff," Jen replied. "And if you could keep

this between the three of us, we sure would appreciate it. At least until after the funeral."

She gave the sheriff a flirtatious wink and he nodded in agreement.

Randy locked the door behind him and watched the sheriff get in his patrol car. As soon as the patrol car pulled away, Randy spun around.

"What the holy hell is going on?" he exclaimed.

"I had to get him out of here," Jen replied.

Randy immediately noticed her Texas accent was gone.

11

Randy was stunned. And confused. The woman in front of him seemed to carry herself differently now. Her warm smile had been replaced by a cold stare.

"Why did you have to get him out of here?" Randy asked. "And how come you're talking funny all of a sudden?"

Jade let out a sigh. She had hoped she could slide in and out of this flea-bitten town quickly and discreetly. But now she not only had run into local law enforcement, her quick shift in alibi had roused the suspicions of Randy. It would be much more efficient if she put down the charade and took care of business.

"Just help me find what I came here for and I'll be on my way," Jade said coldly. "No one has to get hurt."

Randy froze.

"Was someone gonna get hurt?"

Jade reached down and pulled a gun that had been hidden under her jeans in an ankle holster. Randy immediately raised his hands in surrender.

"Stop it," she said. "Just help me find what I came here for."

"Holy Jesus," Randy quivered in a growing panic. "This ain't even my store. Take everything."

"You help me find what I came for and this trigger never gets pulled. Understand?"

Randy nodded, visibly shaken. He pointed to the back corner of the store.

"We... we could start back there," he said.

Jade motioned Randy to the back corner and followed him.

"I still don't understand what I'm looking for," he said. "These are just cheap little figurines."

"You don't really think Clyde made his money selling these things, do you?" she replied.

"I didn't think he made any money at all."

They reached the back of the store and Jade motioned for Randy to start on the bottom shelf and she'd start on the top.

"Your brother was a smuggler, Randy," she explained. "Brought in all kinds of stuff in these little goats."

Randy looked up at her, still not understanding.

"People weren't buying the goats," she continued. "They were buying what was in them."

"Wait. Clyde?" Randy asked. "No way. My brother was no way smart enough to do something like that."

"Oh, he clearly wasn't smart," replied Jade. "Or he'd have been really rich."

E ven though Dean was sitting at his desk, one of many in a maze of gray cubicles, he was a million miles away. Absent-mindedly tapping a pen on his desk, he stared at the data on his computer screen, trying to find any breadcrumb that could put him on Jade's path. He rubbed his tired eyes and looked around his work area for inspiration. But, other than the printout of the blurred photo Dean had shown in his meeting, his cubicle walls were bare. No personal trinkets or mementos from vacations. No family photos or children's drawings. Dean had never married or had children.

Dean sighed. He was almost 55 years old and had absolutely nothing to show for it except this soul-sucking desk job. Not that he hadn't wanted more. He had always craved to be a field agent but was never able to get past the application process. After awhile, he just settled in and took the path of least resistance. Before he knew it, he had clocked in almost thirty numb years and was now staring at early retirement. Maybe it was because of that, or maybe he was having a late-blooming post-mid-life crisis, but he had recently started to grow restless. He had been bringing more and more wild goose chase cases to

Strickland. Looking into odd cold cases. That's how he had discovered Jade.

He looked at the blurry photo of the woman and wondered about who she really was. She probably didn't even have a comfort zone. Traveling the world. Doing whatever the job called for. Assassination? No problem. Theft? She didn't even flinch. Just doing what needed to be done, without being burdened with oppressive moral dilemmas and suffocating mortgage payments.

Normally, this is the part where Dean would just let out a heavy sigh and fall back into the security of his familiar drudgery. But, for some reason, today he resisted. His self-respect finally pushed back. It was time to stop spinning his wheels. This time, he needed to actually do something. To take action and stop waiting for someone to give him permission. It was time to take matters into his own hands.

He grabbed the thick file folder sitting on the side of his desk and opened it, poring over the contents until he found what he was looking for. Grabbing the sheet of paper, he wheeled his chair across the aisle to the cubicle of Agent Kevin Chin.

"I need a favor," Dean said.

"No," Chin responded without looking up from his computer screen.

"I just need you to check something for me," Dean persisted.

He shoved the piece of paper under Chin's chin, giving him no choice in the matter.

"Why can't you do it?" Chin asked.

"Because I'm taking a few personal days," Dean replied.

"Oh, really?" Chin asked, turning to face Dean. "Puttering around the house or going any place interesting?"

"That depends on what you find," Dean replied with a wink.

13

J ade and Randy had worked their way halfway up one of the shelves, turning over every goat in search of a tiny red dot. They worked in tandem, Jade on the top two shelves and Randy on the bottom two, but their styles were very different.

Randy turned over each piece then placed it gingerly back on the shelf. Jade checked quickly then casually tossed the goat aside. Randy flinched every time one broke.

"So you're one of the people my brother worked with?" Randy asked.

Jade didn't answer.

"He was really a smuggler?"

Jade looked down at Randy and nodded.

"Huh," Randy said.

He was almost impressed. His brother had never been much more than a screw-up. Lots of small-time crime but most of that was fueled by too much booze. But a smuggler. An international smuggler, no less. That had a sense of adventure to it that Randy couldn't help but feel a little jealous about.

"So what did he smuggle?" he asked.

But before Jade could answer, they were interrupted by another knock at the store's door. Jade instinctively ducked, pulling Randy down beside her.

"I thought you said nobody shopped here," she whispered. "Can you see who it is?"

"Not from down here," Randy replied.

There was a second knock, more forceful than the first. It clearly wasn't coming from a friendly customer. And they weren't likely to just go away. Jade pulled out her pistol and found a vantage point where she could see through a space in the shelves.

There were two men at the door. The older one was a big man, easily more than six and a half feet tall, with greasy gray hair tucked under a John Deere baseball hat and white stubble covering his round cheeks. The other man was younger and decidedly shorter. But what he lacked in stature he made up for in peculiarity. He had beady eyes and a long, pointed chin. He wore cargo shorts and a camouflage T-shirt with ripped-off sleeves to better display the tattoos covering his wiry arms. But his hair was what really caught your eye. It was cut super short on the side but was long on top and styled into some sort of Mohawk/Pompadour mashup.

"Who are these bozos?" Jade asked.

Randy peered through the space in the shelves.

"Dangit!"

"You know them?" Jade asked.

"Dangit all to hell!" Randy answered. "That's Stonewall and his lapdog, Toby. They're trouble with a capital T."

"Make them go away," Jade said matter of factly.

Randy shook his head.

"You don't understand."

The two men pounded on the door again as Stonewall, the big guy, cupped his hands around his eyes to peer inside.

"They see your truck. They're not going away," Jade said.

"I see your truck, Randy," Stonewall yelled on cue. "I know you're in there."

"Get rid of them. Fast," Jade said, cocking her pistol to make the point.

Randy nodded and took several deep breaths to psyche himself up before popping up and waving at the door.

"Hey guys," he said cheerily.

He unlocked the door and the two men pushed their way in.

"It's about time," Toby, the younger man, said.

"Sorry. I'm doing inventory and had headphones on," Randy stuttered.

"I think you were avoiding me, Randy," said Stonewall.

"Oh, come on. Why would I do that?" Randy asked.

"Because you owe us," said Toby, the younger man with unfortunate hair.

The two men closed in around Randy, backing him up against the counter.

"Look. I told you," Randy said. "I'll get you the money. I just don't have it yet."

He clenched, preparing to take a fist to the face.

"Randy, I've been very patient with you on account of this being Clyde's debt and you just finding out about it and all," said Stonewall. "But my patience is running thin."

"Mine is even thinner," parroted Toby.

"It's only been two days," Randy protested. "I need to liquidate some things. Trust me. You'll get your money."

"That's exactly what your brother used to always say," sneered Stonewall. "Alright. Two more days. But I'm adding an extra one percent service charge. So that's an extra..."

"Three thousand dollars," Toby interrupted.

"Two hundred dollars," Randy argued.

Toby shook his head. "You take me for a fool?"

"You already owe me twenty thousand, boy," said Stonewall.

"Right," replied Randy. "And one percent of twenty thousand is two hundred. Not three thousand."

"You trying to make us believe you only owe us two hundred bucks?" questioned Toby. "That's bullshit."

"No," explained Randy. "I owe you an extra two hundred on top of the twenty thousand dollars. So it's a total of twenty thousand, two hundred."

"Let's just keep it simple and round it up to twenty-five Gs," said Stonewall.

"But that doesn't round up to twenty-five thousand," argued Randy. "That's even more than three thousand."

"You calling me stupid?" snapped Stonewall.

He raised his fist and Randy cowered back, raising his hands to cover his face. Stonewall and Toby laughed then turned to leave.

"Two more days. Twenty-five thousand dollars," Stonewall said as he walked out the door.

Randy quickly flipped the deadbolt. His hand was shaking so violently he could barely turn the lock. He could feel the sweat dripping off his forehead and he was having trouble breathing. He turned to collect himself only to see Jade motioning toward him with her gun.

"We've got work to do," she said, as if nothing had even happened.

Randy let out a deep sigh. *Could this day possibly get any worse?*

14

Viktor Petrov emerged from the non-descript office building on the outskirts of Moscow. He slid on a pair of designer sunglasses and took a deep breath, feeling the warm June sun on his face. It was a sunny morning and milder weather had already begun to make the long, wet winter a distant memory. But Viktor wasn't appreciating the weather. He was thinking about his little brother. Their entire life, Anton had been the fun-loving goof who could always make his serious older brother laugh. In fact, he took pride in cracking the cold facade of his sibling. Viktor had sometimes acted annoyed but they both knew he secretly loved it. And now he was gone. Because of HER.

The thought of Jade quickly pushed Viktor's memories away to make room for a growing anger. Jade had stolen from him before and was a constant thorn in his side. That's why he had begun taking extra precautions. Shipping through new sources and hiding the books at the one place where no one would ever think to find them: his brother's apartment.

The Koslov twins came out of the office building. Leo, the

tie-less one with the snake tattoo, was still wiping blood from his hands with a wet handkerchief.

Without looking back at them, Viktor began walking briskly toward a black limousine, the Koslov twins stepping quickly to keep up.

"You think it was her?" Leo asked in Russian.

"I have no doubt," Viktor answered.

"You think she knows about the goat?" Leo pressed.

Viktor responded with a cold stare as he reached the limo and waited for one of the twins to open the rear door for him.

"So, what do we do?" Peter asked, opening the car door.

Viktor smiled, his lips curling into a devilish, slimy grin.

"I assume she knows about the goat and is going to retrieve it. So we will also go to the goat," he said.

The smile vanished from his face and he slid in the back-seat, followed by the two hulking men.

"We keep her from stealing the merchandise," he contin-ued. "And we avenge my brother's death."

Leo tapped on the tinted privacy glass that separated the driver from the rear of the limo and the limo began to move forward.

"This will be fun," Leo said with a grin.

"Fun?" Peter questioned.

"I've never been to Texas."

15

Jade and Randy had progressed to the second shelf in The Lazy Goat. Working on the bottom shelves, Jade continued to toss her rejected figurines to the ground, sometimes breaking them, while Randy tried to be as careful as possible while he searched the higher shelves.

"So, what exactly is in the goat?" Randy asked casually, as if it were just too friends out on a shopping trip.

Not feeling any need to be cordial, Jade didn't answer. Instead, she continued to check each figurine then toss it aside.

"I bet it's drugs. Right?" Randy guessed. "Or a computer chip. With some sort of secret weapon recipe or something."

Jade shot a glare at Randy, signaling him to shut him up. But Randy didn't catch the visual cue and continued his guessing game.

"You'll at least tell me if I'm warm, right?" he asked. "A map? Jewels? A key to a safety deposit box?"

Jade snapped, her patience completely run down. She yanked the pistol from behind her back and pushed the barrel up against Randy's nose.

"I will tell you absolutely nothing," she seethed. "And you will say absolutely nothing in return. Got it?"

Randy nodded meekly. Having made her point, Jade pulled the gun away and returned to the figurines.

"It's just that, the more I know, the more I'll be able to help you find it," Randy persisted.

"You're doing fine."

"But what if it's not here?" Randy asked. "Maybe Clyde hid it. How would you know where to look next?

Jade stopped. She had been moving so fast and furiously, she had barely considered the fact that she didn't know where else to look.

"You'll tell me where to look," she answered, a hint of a threat in her reply.

"It'd be easier, for you, if I showed you." Randy bargained. "People around here don't take too kindly to strangers. I could help bridge the gap."

"First off, I don't care if they take kindly to me or not. I'm not here to make friends. Secondly, why are you even offering?"

Randy shrugged.

"Sooner you find what you need, the sooner you move on. Plus, I could use the distraction."

"You think this is a game?"

"No. It seems pretty dangerous. But the way I see it, you're less likely to shoot me if I can help you, so why not help? Besides, it's not like I'm hurting Clyde. He's dead. I'm just fixing his screw-ups."

Jade thought about the offer. On the one hand, it could speed things along if she had an inside man to help. On the other, she couldn't really trust him and she preferred to work alone. But he had nothing to gain by helping. Unless...

"I'm not giving you a cut," she said.

"Don't want it. I'd just rather help you than have you go around threatening everyone in town."

The conversation was interrupted by another loud BANG at the door.

"You've got to be kidding me!" she exclaimed in frustration.

Randy looked toward the door. "Oh, shit. It's Mama."

"Your mother?" Jade asked.

"Who else am I gonna call mama?" he asked. "I better get it."

Jade grabbed the back of Randy's belt loop, holding him in place.

"Well, I can't just ignore her," Randy protested.

"You can. And you will."

The unmistakable jingle of keys could be heard from the other side of the door and before Jade could even react, the door burst open. Jade pulled Randy down as she watched the large woman in her late 60s barge into the room. Weighing 250 pounds with long silver hair pulled up in a giant bun on the top of her head and dressed in a blindingly bright floral tunic that billowed over equally bright yellow pants, Mama was not one you could easily ignore. Her presence was so dominating, Jade barely noticed the peculiar, tiny old woman that walked in behind her.

"I gotta pee," the tiny woman announced.

From her crooked, auburn wig and garish costume jewelry, the little woman was clearly a fan of accessories...and makeup. Lots of makeup.

Randy looked at Jade, unsure what to do. Resigned to the interruption and not wanting a massacre just yet, Jade motioned for Randy to talk to them.

"Hey, Mama! Hi, Pauline," Randy said as he popped up from behind the shelf. "What are y'all doing here?"

"Your Aunt Pauline needs to go to the bathroom," Mama answered. "And I want to meet this lady friend of yours."

Shocked and unsure what to do, Randy looked back in Jade's direction.

Randy stammered. "How do you–"

"Sheriff told me all about her," Mama said matter-of-factly. "Now where is she?"

Jade's stomach dropped as she played out a thousand ways to handle the situation. The easiest solution would be to just shoot them all, find her goat and be on her way. But Randy had been right. There was the outside chance the figurine wasn't in the store and she could use his help to track it down. If she killed his mother, he probably wouldn't be as easy to work with.

What am I even thinking? she thought to herself. *I work alone.*

She took a deep breath and grabbed her gun.

16

J ade stood up from behind the shelf, catching the attention of Randy and Mama. She saw the fear in Randy's eyes and the shock in Mama's. As she hid her gun on a shelf, she smiled, immediately sliding into her southern belle persona.

"Hi. I'm Jen," she said with her Texas twang. "Jen Brown."

Mama stared at the blonde beauty walking toward her. For once in her life, she was actually speechless. Jade extended her hand as she approached the big woman. Mama looked at it and shook her head.

"You put that hand down, Jen Brown," she said, extending both of her big bear arms. "You give Mama a big Texas hug."

Before Jen could respond, she was pulled into a death grip. She struggled to breathe as Mama squeezed her tight for an uncomfortably long time. Finally, the big woman let her go, taking a step back to take in Jade like a show pony.

"Randy, you wanna explain why you've been keeping this beautiful young woman from your mama?" she said, never taking her eyes off Jade.

"I don't–"

"We just wanted to make sure it was real before we made it official," Jade interrupted. "You know how online dating can be."

"I do not, thank the Lord," Mama replied. "Call me old-fashioned, but I don't believe the Good Lord meant for machines to be matchmakers. But I do appreciate you coming to help bury my poor boy."

She hung her head in reverence, allowing herself a moment of vulnerability before snapping back to her tough-as-nails persona as the tiny woman re-emerged from the backroom.

"You ain't got no toilet paper," the woman said matter-of-factly.

"There's plenty of toilet paper, Aunt Pauline" Randy argued.

Pauline shrugged. "I used a towel."

She turned her coke-bottle-thick glasses in Jade's direction and a wide grin spread across her face, revealing lipstick stains on her teeth.

"Is this her?" she asked, walking over to Jade, giving her a thorough once over. "Dang-it-all to pieces. Ain't you a pretty piece of candy?"

"Thank you," Jade responded, unsure of what else to say.

"We were fixing to go to Perty's," Mama said. "You two lovebirds should come with us."

"No, I wouldn't want to impose," Jade protested.

"She just got here and we're trying to clean up the store, Mama," Randy offered.

"Well, we'll just wait for ya then," Mama said.

"It could take a while," Jade said.

Mama reached over and pinched Jade's cheeks. The thief had to fight her defensive reflex to punch Mama in the throat and throw her to the ground.

"That's okay," Mama said. "It'll give us lots of time to visit."

Jade smiled and pulled Randy aside, quietly demanding he get rid of his relatives immediately.

"You want to help? Get rid of them," Jade whispered.

"I can't just tell my Mama to leave," Randy whispered back.

"You're not really comprehending the seriousness of this situation, are you?" Jade asked.

"Can't we just leave them out of it?" Randy argued.

"I never wanted them in it!"

Randy looked over at his mother and Pauline.

"This could be a good thing," Randy said.

"Get rid of them."

"Mama knew Clyde better than anyone. She knows things that I don't even know. I bet if you got her talking about him, you could find out all sorts of information that could help you find what you're looking for."

Jade seemed to be thinking about it, so Randy sweetened the deal.

"We get them to the restaurant. You can talk to Mama and once you get what you need, we excuse ourselves and come back. Trust me. Once Mama knows food is coming, she ain't gonna get up."

Jade looked over at the two women. Mama was fussing with Pauline's wig, trying to straighten it. Realizing it was the least violent option, Jade let out yet another sigh and nodded.

"You're either extremely gutsy or incredibly stupid," she said. "But if you try to pull anything at all, your mother goes first. Then the clown lady. Then you. Got it?"

17

Agent Chin leaned forward at his desk, shoveling the last bite of reheated spaghetti into his mouth. Part of him was kicking himself for agreeing to help Dean. Now he was stuck at his desk waiting for the information Dean needed. Still, he had to admit that it was a little exciting. He wasn't sure what Dean had up his sleeve, but it involved finding unauthorized information on the Russian mob so it had to be something good. And a little under-the-table espionage work would break up the monotony of the day (which was spent doing government-sanctioned espionage work).

As he wiped stray sauce from his face with a paper napkin, his phone pinged with a text notification.

Finally, he thought to himself.

It was from Agent Steve Relinski, who worked at the FBI office in Moscow. Chin and Relinski trained at Quantico together and had casually kept in touch over the years. Still, Relinski had been a little surprised to hear from Chin, though not that surprised about who he was asking about. Viktor Petrov had been a person of interest of the FBI for years.

Relinski had been intrigued by Chin's request to keep

things on the downlow. However, he was never one to question the secretive processes of the bureau and he knew Chin could be trusted. Besides, truth be told, he enjoyed having a somewhat covert assignment for a change. He thought working on a counter-terrorism unit in Russia would be filled with excitement. It turned out, as was true of almost every other law enforcement job, it was primarily paperwork. On the plus side, it was a small Moscow branch, which made it easier for him to get the information Chin requested.

Chin read Relinski's text then carried his phone down the hall to an empty conference room.

18

A fter putting in his vacation request, Dean had gone back to his apartment to prepare for a trip. All he needed was the destination.

The modest apartment had come pre-furnished and Dean had done nothing to add to it. In fact, at a glance, you'd wonder if it was even occupied. There were no signs of life. No books on shelves. No framed photos or personal affects to be seen. The small kitchen seemed as if no one ever cooked in it. Any food, plates and cooking utensils were stored out of view.

The kitchen opened up into a living room that consisted of nothing more than a dated, green couch, a faux-wood coffee table, two empty bookshelves and the only sign of occupancy: a 42-inch TV on a black TV stand.

It wasn't that Dean had no personality, it was just that he never really moved in. It was supposed to be a temporary situation until he could find something he really liked. Then, a week turned into a month which turned into a year. It was his fully-furnished comfort zone. Routine. Low maintenance. And boring. He'd been fine with that for years. But lately, the boredom had started to eat at him. Maybe it was some of the

FBI procedural shows he had started watching, or maybe it was his pending birthday. Either way, he had begun to want more out of his career. And his life.

His restlessness had led him toward his fascination with Jade. Or maybe it was the other way around. Jade was everything Dean wasn't. Brazen. Bold. And not afraid to live on the edge. Not that he was completely seduced by her lifestyle. She was a cold-blooded killer and thief and needed to be stopped. Still, chasing after her would give Dean a chance to step into her exciting world. And bringing her down could change everyone's perception of him at the bureau.

Dean walked through the small living room into his bedroom. The afternoon sun shone through the faded yellow curtains, casting a pale yellow glow over the maroon bedspread. He opened the sliding doors of his bedroom closet and pulled a black leather travel bag from a shelf. Still unsure where he might be going, he began to fill the bag with a few changes of clothes.

He had walked into his bathroom to grab a few toiletries when he heard his phone ring. Rushing back into the bedroom, he snatched the phone up and checked the Caller ID. It was Special Agent Chin.

"Yeah?" Dean answered.

"Your pal is making a move," Chin replied. "He's headed to the airport."

"I knew it. Do you know where he's going?"

"Not yet. But we'll know soon enough, and I'll call you back. You ready to tell me what this is all about?"

"It may be nothing," Dean replied. "But I need you to do one more thing."

19

Randy's truck pulled into the crowded Perty's parking lot. Even though it was practically across the street from The Lazy Goat, there was no way Mama was going to walk it.

"That's not how a dignified person arrives to an eating establishment," she had argued.

So Randy, Mama, Pauline and Jade had crammed into his pickup to make the thirty-second drive across the street.

When Jade saw all of the cars in front of the restaurant, her stomach dropped again. Now there would be even more witnesses. Thankful that she had chosen a blonde wig and a little extra makeup as part of her disguise, she hoped it would be enough to protect the identity she had worked so hard at keep hidden. Part of her power was her anonymity. Without that, it would be harder for her to slide in and out of people's lives on assignment.

She assured herself she was fine. This was a small town in the middle of nowhere. And, if all went as planned, she would be in and out before the day ended. A blip in their tiny little lives that would fade from memory before anyone would even know to ask any questions. Besides, it was a risk she would have to take. According to Randy, his mother could hold key information. She could tell from their brief time together that force and threats weren't going to work with this tough lady. She needed to win her trust. And the quickest way to win over a person is to buy them a meal. So Jade had not only agreed to join Mama and Pauline for dinner, but to also pay for it.

She quickly slid out of the crammed truck, turning to watch Randy help his larger mother and small aunt. Once on her feet, Mama smoothed out her house dress and pointed to Jade.

"Randall, you escort your lady friend inside like a gentleman. There's people watching."

Randy held out a hand to Jade, who looked at it incredulously. Nodding in embarrassment, he pulled it back and opened the restaurant door for Mama, Pauline and finally Jade.

The smell of greasy food and hot coffee engulfed them immediately. The restaurant was as packed as Jade had feared. She scanned the dining area. A dozen red tables were all occupied. So were five of the six booths that lined the wall. Jade nudged Randy and pointed to the one lone booth at the back of the restaurant by the bathroom doors.

Mama had already spotted the empty booth and couldn't have been happier. Its location would ensure she would have to parade through the entire restaurant so everyone would see her. Pauline trotted behind Mama, then Randy. Jade followed them all, her head down to avoid eye contact with anyone.

There was a wide range of people in the restaurant. Large families ignoring their crying babies and whining toddlers. Elderly couples sitting in silence. A group of teenagers laughing at images on their phones.

Several people stopped to offer their sympathies to Mama. Jade noticed she had assumed a grieving mother's posture, nodding to her well-wishers with a sense of sorrow that completely contradicted the bright and sunny outfit she was wearing.

Mama stopped to accept the sympathies of a group of older women sitting at one table. The way they all spoke, Jade gathered this was her beehive and she prepared herself to be introduced. But much to her surprise, Mama continued past them toward the booth. Jade noticed how the women immediately turned to each other in conspiratorial whispers.

Looks like everyone's got a false face, she thought to herself.

They finally reached the booth and sat down. Pauline slid in first and Mama pulled in next to her. Jade insisted on sliding into her side of the booth first, putting her as far out of view as possible. She grabbed a large red plastic Perty's menu sitting on the table and buried her face inside of it.

Mama was reveling in her moment.

"Did you see the look on those old taters' faces?" she said. "June looked as confused as a fart in a fan factory."

She reached across the table and pulled Jade's menu down.

"Don't hide that pretty face of yours, sweetheart" she chided. "If I looked like you, I'd be holding my head so high they'd have to tie it down."

Mama smiled at Jade proudly then looked at the people sitting in the restaurant. Jade followed Mama's gaze to see that practically everyone was pretending not to look at them. She quickly snapped back around, raising the menu up again.

"So much for slipping in and out," she mumbled to herself.

"What's that?" Mama asked.

"I said it's probably been so long since you've been out."

Mama nodded as Randy passed menus out to everyone else. Pauline stared at hers and made a weird smacking sound with her lips. Recognizing the curious sound, Mama looked over at her big sister.

"Pauline, where are your teeth?"

"They fell out in the truck," Pauline answered with a shrug.

"Honey, you can't eat when you don't have no teeth in your mouth," Mama said.

"I can't eat when she don't have her teeth in her mouth," Randy interjected. "I'll go get 'em."

He scooted out of the booth. Jade watched him go and thought this may be a good time to make her exit, too.

"I'll go help him," she offered, sliding out of the booth.

Mama grabbed her arm.

"Don't you be silly," Mama said. "You stay here so we can have a little girl talkin' time."

Jade looked into Mama's intimidating eyes.

Was she suspicious?

She reluctantly slid back into the booth. She had left her gun in the shop. There was no way to grab it discreetly. But she had already instinctively surveyed her surroundings and spotted nearly a dozen items that could double as a weapon if she needed them.

20

"So how long have you known my Randall?" Mama asked in a tone that made the friendly girl talk immediately feel more like an inquisition.

Jade could tell Mama had a pretty good bullshit detector. No doubt a product of growing up a strong woman in the man's world of East Texas, especially in the fifties and sixties. She had probably spent a lifetime navigating lies and other obstacles meant to keep her in her place. She clearly knew how to hold her own and was not easily fooled. Or intimidated. It made for a strong woman, but a potential problem for Jade.

"We've only been together a few weeks," Jade answered, pouring on as much Southern charm as she could. "But I feel like I've known him my whole life."

Mama nodded knowingly.

"That's what happens when it's the right one," she said before leaning forward to drive her next question home. "Unless you're just desperate for a husband."

Jade laughed sheepishly. "Oh my, no," she said. "I'd only gone on that dating site on a lark. Randy just took me by surprise. I assure you, I'm not a husband hunter. By the way, I'm so sorry to hear about your son."

Jade winced at the awkward, sudden change of topic, but Mama didn't seem to notice.

"Thank you so much, Hun," Mama said. "A mama should never have to bury her own child. It's a burden I wouldn't wish on my worst enemy."

"Except Dixie," Pauline interrupted.

Mama looked at her sister, confused, so Pauline offered an explanation.

"You said you wish Dixie's son were dead just so she could feel what you're going through."

"You must have misheard me," Mama replied.

"You know I didn't," Pauline answered defiantly.

"Were you and Clyde close?" Jade asked, trying to steer the conversation back to something useful.

"My Clyde was a real mama's boy," Mama said. "He'd watch Wheel of Fortune most every night with me. He took good care of his mama."

"Did he live in town?" Jade asked.

"Just outside of town," Mama replied. "He and Randy both."

"He lived with Randy?"

"They both live with me," Mama replied. "Didn't Randy tell you?"

Before Jade could think of an answer, a young woman walked up to their table.

21

Amy Jo Billings was a pretty woman in her mid-twenties with a lot of blonde hair and not a lot of clothes.

"Hey there, Mama. Hi, Miss Pauline," she said between smacks of gum.

"Amy Jo," Mama answered flatly, not even trying to hide her disdain.

"You had to get out, too, huh?" Amy Jo asked, oblivious to Mama's attitude. "I hear ya. I just couldn't stay cooped up in the house any longer. Everything there reminds me of my Clyde."

Her lip quivered in what Jade recognized as a well-rehearsed act of sorrow.

"That's cuz it's all his stuff," Mama replied sarcastically.

"The life of a widow can be so lonely," Amy Jo went on. "I know you understand."

So, Clyde was married, Jade thought to herself.

It was information that hadn't shown up in her research of the redneck trafficker.

"I don't care how lonely you are," Mama replied. "Just try to keep your legs together until we bury him."

Once again ignoring Mama's comment, Amy Jo turned to Jade.

"Hi. I'm Amy Jo. Clyde's wife."

"EX-wife," Mama corrected.

"No, ma'am," Amy Jo said. "He never filed the papers."

"I'm Jen," Jade said. "So sorry for your loss."

"Thank you," Amy Jo answered. "That's so sweet of you."

"Jen is Randall's new girlfriend," Mama interjected.

"No shit?" Amy Jo said, making no effort to hide her shock. "Good for him."

Before Mama could respond with an insult, a woman in a short denim skirt and skin-tight camisole walked over to the table.

"Come on," the woman said to Amy Jo, confirming their connection. "It's 2-for-1 at Willy's."

"Don't go gettin' prissy, Missy," Amy Jo chastised. "I'll meet you outside."

The friend groaned loudly and pouted off while Amy Jo turned her attention back to Mama.

"I really should be going, though," she said. "I have wounds that need healing."

"Is that what you're calling it these days?" Mama retorted.

Amy Jo turned to Jade.

"Will you be at the funeral?" she asked.

Mama answered before Jade had a chance to say anything.

"You bet your barely covered ass she will."

Amy Jo nodded, letting Mama's surly attitude roll off her bare shoulders.

"Well, I guess I'll see you there then," she said with a shrug.

She strutted away, catching the gaze of every man in the restaurant.

"That little tramp's got some nerve showing her dumplings around here," Mama grumbled.

"Her dress was so short I could see her religion," Pauline added with a toothless grin.

"So, she's Clyde's wife?" Jade asked, curious about another potential lead on the missing goat figurine.

"Ex-wife. I don't care what papers he didn't file. She left my Clyde high and dry nearly two years ago," Mama answered.

"She's a dancer," Pauline offered.

"I guarantee you there ain't much dancing in what she does," Mama corrected.

"I thought she was pretty good," Pauline argued.

Mama slapped Pauline's hand. "You ain't never been to one of those places where she works."

"You don't know where I've been," Pauline snapped back.

She looked at Jade and spoke in a conspiratorial whisper. "I've seen things."

"So, Clyde hadn't seen her for two years?" Jade asked, steering the conversation back to her question.

"And now she shows up here acting like a poor lonely widow just to get some attention."

So much for the ex-wife, Jade thought.

But knowing that Clyde lived with his mother, and with Randy, was very useful information. Thinking of Randy, she turned around to see what was taking him so long. She could see him through the front windows of the restaurant, on his hands and knees, reaching under the truck for what was probably Pauline's teeth.

Jade felt the vibration of her phone. Someone was texting her and she was pretty sure who it was.

22

"Excuse me," Jade said, sliding out of the booth. "I need to go to the ladies' room."

Before Mama or Pauline could respond, Jade had stepped into the hallway that led to the restrooms. As she had hoped, there was a third door that led into the kitchen. Jade pushed it open and walked quickly between the racks of food and sizzling stovetops until she found a back exit.

Jade stepped outside and read the text that simply said STATUS?

Jade dialed the number for the sender of the text.

"Do you have it?" Donovan Fontaine asked immediately, skipping any perfunctory salutation.

"Not yet," Jade answered. "But I'm close."

"Good. Get in. Get out. Viktor Petrov is headed your way."

Jade's pulse quickened. She figured he would be hot on her trail but was hoping it would take a few days. She should have hidden Anton's body to buy her time, but it's not easy to sneak a 230-lb. corpse out of a luxury hotel with a bodyguard right outside the door.

"You still have time," Donovan said, as if reading her mind.

"He and a couple of his enforcers just left and they have a layover in New York City. They won't even arrive in Texas until sometime tomorrow."

"I'll be long gone by then," Jade replied, feeling reassured.

"Remember, Jade. No messes."

"I'll do what I need to do."

"You'll do what I pay you to do. I don't want to draw any more attention to this than you already have. It's bad enough you've got Petrov involved. Dead bodies are bad for business."

He hung up before Jade could argue his point. Which was just as well, because she really didn't have much of an argument. She cleared the record of the call and the text from her phone and stuck it in her back pocket.

She could tell she wasn't going to get anywhere with Mama. It was time she got back to work at The Lazy Goat. She walked around to the front of the restaurant just in time to see Randy retrieving a pair of teeth from under the truck. He stood and wiped them on his shirt. Not satisfied, he leaned into his truck and grabbed a rag to clean them.

"Randy," she yelled out.

Randy looked up and she waved him over.

"What are you doing out here?" he asked as he got closer.

"Let's go," she said, motioning toward The Lazy Goat.

"We can't go yet," he protested. "We haven't even ordered."

"As much as I enjoy this redneck dinner from hell, I've got a job to do. And I'm running out of patience. You do not want me to run out of patience."

Randy nodded, but looked back inside the restaurant.

"If we abandon Mama and Aunt Pauline in there, they'll just come back to the shop and make things worse."

Jade sighed. She should have just tied them up in the store when she had the chance.

"Give me the store keys," she demanded.

Randy started to argue, but Jade interrupted him.

"I'm not negotiating with you," she snapped.

Randy nodded and dug for the keys in his pocket. Needing both hands, he held out Pauline's teeth for Jade to hold. Reluctantly, she accepted.

Randy found the keys and traded them for the teeth.

"That's got my truck keys on there," he said.

"Good. You're not going anywhere until I find what I'm looking for," she answered. "Now give me your phone."

Randy handed over his cell phone.

"If you try anything, if you say anything to anyone, if the cops show up or anything so much as even looks suspicious, I will track you down and kill you all. Got it?"

Randy nervously nodded in acknowledgement.

"I need you to go inside and order with everyone. Keep them occupied and out of my hair. If all goes well, I'll find what I need and be out of your hair before you're finished eating."

"You sure you don't need my help?" he asked.

She patted him on the cheek.

"Only if I don't find it."

Jade meant it as a threat, but Randy smiled and nodded as if it were an offer.

"Check behind the counter," Randy said with a smile. "Sometimes Clyde would store some stuff there."

Jade nodded and ran across the street. She heard Randy calling out to her.

"Good luck!"

23

Dean drove his dark blue Chevy Sonic down Interstate 395 toward Ronald Reagan Airport. He still wasn't even sure where he would be going, but wanted to be ready as soon as he had the information he needed.

The muffled sound of his cell phone began to ring, and Dean fumbled through the coat pockets of his suit jacket until he finally found it.

"Yeah?" he answered without even looking at the Caller ID.

"He's headed to Dallas," Agent Chin answered.

"You're sure?" Dean asked.

"Caught a flight to DFW a few hours ago."

"A few hours ago?" Dean asked, pushing his foot on the gas pedal.

"Relax," Chin said. "It's a sixteen-hour flight. You've still got a big jump on him."

Dean spotted the sign for the airport exit.

"Were you able to get the export manifest?" Dean asked.

"It's not that easy, Dean. I'm still working on it."

"Sorry. I appreciate the help," Dean said. "I've got to go. I need to call the Dallas office to see if we can get any more intel on where he's heading in Texas."

Dean heard the groan on the other end of the line and smiled.

"No way," Chin said. "I'm invested now. I'll look into it. But Dean, this guy's dangerous. You're gonna need backup."

"I'm not after Petrov," Dean replied. "I'm after who he's leading me to."

24

"What do you mean she left?" Mama snapped.

Randy shrugged, trying not to watch as Pauline fumbled to get her dentures in her mouth.

"She got a call and had to go," Randy answered. "Some emergency."

"And she didn't even have the decency to say goodbye?" Mama asked.

A thought dawned on her and she leaned forward, glaring at her son.

"What did you do?" she demanded. "Did you make her mad?"

"I didn't do anything!" Randy argued.

"Did you get fresh with her?" Pauline asked with a devilish grin.

"I didn't touch her," Randy said. "She just had to get her things from the store and head out. I'm sorry."

"Maybe you should've got fresh with her," Pauline argued.

"Well, she's coming back for the funeral, ain't she?" Mama asked.

Randy shook his head and avoided eye contact. It was hard to lie to his mother and he had never been able to get away with it. But now, their lives depended on it.

"I don't know. Maybe."

Mama sized up her son, weighing his words.

"I don't know what to tell you, Mama," Randy said with a tired sigh.

"Don't you take an attitude with me, boy," Mama snapped. "I'll jerk a knot in your tail so fast-"

Her threat was interrupted by the arrival of a teenage girl in a maroon polo shirt with the Perty's logo silkscreened over the left chest.

"Y'all know what y'all want?" she asked, holding her pen to a notepad.

Mama immediately switched her attention to the waitress.

"I'll have the Perty's special. Extra gravy. And she'll have the chicken sandwich, but could you put the fries on the side. They're gonna be for me."

"I want an ice cream cone, too," Pauline added.

"For dessert," Mama said.

"That's all I want," Pauline argued.

The waitress looked at Mama, who nodded in approval, then turned to a distracted Randy.

"I don't know," he said. "Just a burger."

"What kind of burger?" the waitress asked.

"I don't care."

"Well, you have to tell me what kind," the waitress said. "We've got lots of different burgers. There's the Perty Burger. Perty Bacon Burger. The Perty Supreme Burger. Perty Chili Cheeseburger. Perty Ranch Burger. Perty Jalepeño Bacon Ranch Supreme Burger."

"Just pick one," Randy interrupted.

The waitress froze, unsure what to do.

"You want me to just pick one?" she asked.

"Yeah. Just give me your favorite."

"Oh, I don't eat burgers," the waitress said. "I'm a vegetarian."

Mama shook her head, being very obvious about her disapproval.

"Just give me what she's having," Randy said.

Relieved to have an answer, the waitress nodded and walked away. Mama leaned forward.

"Did you hear that?" she whispered loudly for everyone to hear. "A vegetarian. Right out in the open with no shame whatsoever. First your girlfriend runs out on us and now this. This day's gone from bad to worse."

"Don't forget Clyde died," Pauline chimed in.

"How could I forget that, Pauline?" Mama yelled, directing her frustration at her sister.

Randy pressed his index fingers into his temples, hoping to relieve the pressure that was building up fast.

Maybe it was all over, he thought. *Maybe when we're done eating, she'll be long out of town and we can just go home and it will be like none of this ever happened.*

But even at the thought it, he couldn't deny that he felt a little bit of disappointment. He was actually looking forward to the little adventure. At least it was something different.

When the waitress returned with their food, Randy smiled politely, faking his happiness for the sake of politeness. However, as he was digging into his Perty's Special, the sheriff's patrol car was pulling into the parking lot of The Lazy Goat.

25

Taking up where she had left off, Jade flipped the figurines over quickly and methodically, unceremoniously tossing them aside after she inspected them. She had wished the wall of windows had shades. Instead, she had to work in the dark, relying solely on the illuminating glow of the neon goat head that hung in one of the windows.

She worked fast. Without all the interruptions, she was able to move through the shelves quickly. Randy and his family weren't likely to wait around the restaurant forever and she had to be prepared for them to return to the shop after.

The fact that she was even having to deal with Randy and team grated on her. Normally, she would never have allowed for so much exposure. She would have come stealthily at night and found her assignment before anyone had even known she was there. At the very least, she would have found out all she could about Clyde Philpot's family before she arrived and done a better job of containing the situation. But she didn't have that kind of time. Fortunately, now that she was able to work alone, she should be able to find the contraband quickly and slip out of town

As she checked the last handful of goats, she became aware of someone else's presence. Not turning around to arouse suspicion, she continued working, but her attention was now focused on her surroundings. The slightest sound or movement was all she needed. Then she felt a movement. Someone was behind her...approaching slowly. Jade waited until she could sense they were close enough and then, in one lightning-fast motion, she spun around, grabbed her assailant by the arm and flipped him. As she had anticipated, he had been pointing a gun at her and she knocked it from his hand mid-flip, sending it clattering into the shelves and on to the carpet ten feet away. His body hit the floor with a thud and Jade, still holding on to his arm, had swung around so her knee was pinned on his chest.

That's the same time that Jade realized her attacker was Sheriff McKinley.

"Damn you, Randy," she muttered under her breath.

But she immediately noticed the confused look on the sheriff's face. He clearly wasn't expecting to see her. Which meant Randy may not have tipped him off. In a split-second instinctive move, she decided to play dumb.

"Oh my God," she said in her twang. "I am so sorry!"

The sheriff tried to hide the pain as she helped him to his feet.

"I thought you were an attacker," Jade said.

"I thought you were robbing the place," Sheriff McKinley said.

He walked over to his gun and placed it back in his holster.

"Those were some pretty fancy moves," he said.

"I took a self-defense course," Jade said, trying to disarm any suspicion with a big smile.

The sheriff studied her, not quite sure if he bought her story. He also needed a moment to get his bearings. The fall had really clocked him.

"Can I ask you what you're doing here?" he said, looking at the destruction all around him.

"Just helping Randy with the inventory," she offered. "He took Mama and Aunt Pauline across the street to dinner."

"Inventory?" the sheriff asked, focusing on the first part of her explanation. "I thought he was gonna sell the place."

"He is, but no sense letting all this go to waste, right?" Jade replied. "Thank the Lord for eBay."

"For just taking inventory, you sure are destroying a lot of these little...things," the sheriff pointed out.

"Randy told me which ones were worthless and to destroy them as I go," Jade said. "Makes it easier to sort them later. I know. It sounded weird to me, too."

She needed to change the subject.

"Why are you here?" she asked. "The front door is locked."

"I let myself in the back door. It's had a broken lock for as long as I've been sheriff," he explained.

"Thought you'd treat yourself to some of the merchandise?" Jade said with a wink.

The sheriff was offended by the joke.

"I don't steal, ma'am," he replied. "I saw movement inside and I was checking it out."

He told Jade that he knew Clyde dealt with some very suspicious types and wanted to make sure that didn't play a part in his death.

"You think his death wasn't an accident?" Jade asked, pretending to sound aghast.

"He definitely died from pissing on a transformer," the sheriff replied. "But who does that, seriously? Even when they're as drunk as Clyde was."

"You think someone forced him to pee on the transformer?" Jade asked, trying not to sound too sarcastic.

Sheriff McKinley turned red. When he heard his theory said out loud, he had to admit it did sound a little bizarre.

"I have to consider all possibilities," he finally answered.

Now it was his turn to change the subject.

"So Randy just let you come over here all by yourself?"

"Why? You don't think I'm trustworthy?" she asked.

"I don't trust anyone," he replied. "Probably why I went into law enforcement. Randy, on the other hand, would trust a fox in a hen house."

He stared at Jade, looking for any chink in her armor. But Jade met his stare with her own. And while she continued to attempt to disarm him with her smile, she was deciding whether or not to get rid of him before he could cause any problems.

Their stare-down was rudely interrupted by the flash and flicker of the overhead fluorescents turning on. They both snapped their heads around to see who had joined them.

J ade didn't know whether to feel relieved or annoyed by the three familiar figures standing in the store's doorway. Even though her eyes had to adjust to the sudden burst of light, the body shapes alone were enough to identify the new arrivals. Randy's voice all but confirmed it.

"Sheriff! What are you doing here?" he screeched.

Randy looked at Jade with panic in his eyes and shook his head to try and tell her he wasn't the reason the sheriff was there.

"I didn't call you or anything," he said to the sheriff, driving his point home.

"Just making my rounds," Sheriff McKinley said. "Thought you were being robbed."

"We had to eat without you," Mama chided Jade.

"I didn't get my ice cream," Pauline added.

The sheriff ignored Mama and Pauline and motioned toward Jade.

"She tells me you told her to come over here..."

Randy froze. Clearly Jade had made up some story for the sheriff. His thoughts began to whirl. What if he told the truth?

The sheriff could get the upper hand quick enough and then this whole nightmare would be over. But then he noticed how Jade was standing behind the sheriff, her hand behind her back, and he realized she probably had her hand on her gun. There was no way the sheriff could react fast enough. She had them cornered.

"But you seemed a little surprised to see her," the sheriff continued.

"What? No," Randy stammered. "I was surprised to see YOU. I knew SHE would be here. I told her to come here. She has permission to be here and it's nothing weird or anything, I promise."

"You were supposed to pay for dinner," Mama said to Jade again, uninterested in her son's nervous rambling.

Jade seized the opportunity to shift attention away from Randy.

"I'm sorry, ma'am," Jade replied. "I just had to take care of some things and get my stuff and time just ran away from me."

"What was the emergency?" Mama asked.

"You told me you were helping Randy with the inventory," the sheriff said.

Jade cursed herself. Clearly, she and Randy had provided different alibis. She should have made sure they were synced up earlier. She never tripped up her alibis. This whole redneck family was throwing her off.

"Well, I was," she said to the sheriff with a flirty smile. "I got a call from my mother and she said it was an emergency and I needed to come home, so I came to get my stuff and..."

"What kind of emergency?" Mama asked.

Jade didn't miss a beat. "She has some gastric bowel issues and was out of her medication..."

She let the statement linger so everyone could use their own worst imagination. No one likes to talk about bowel issues, she had learned. It's an instant way to shut down questions.

"What kind?" Mama asked, clearly not aware of the rule of not talking about bowel issues. "I got the IBS. You don't wanna be anywhere around if I miss my pills for a couple of days."

"I'm not sure," Jade replied. "She doesn't like to talk about it. But anyway, it doesn't matter. Right before I left, my mother called me back to tell me she found her pills and everything was alright. But, since I was here, I thought I'd surprise Randy by doing a little bit of the inventory for him. He's got so much on his mind with his brother's funeral and all."

"God rest his soul," Mama moaned, remembering she was in mourning.

Randy walked over to Jade and gave her a hug.

"You are such a sweetheart," he said. "That was so thoughtful of you."

He turned to face the sheriff, keeping his arm around Jade. Even under the circumstances, he couldn't help but notice how good it felt to have his arm around such a beautiful woman. For a split second, he found himself lost in the charade, leaning into his 'girlfriend' and kissing her on the forehead.

The sheriff never took his eyes off of Jade, but she played along with Randy's affection without a hiccup.

"Be careful putting your arm around her," the sheriff said. "She'll put you on the floor in a heartbeat."

"Randy honey, I need to show you something real quick," Jade said, pulling Randy away from the sheriff.

As soon as they were out of earshot, and with their back to everyone, she whispered to him.

"You're holding out on me."

"Holding out how?" he whispered back.

Knowing they had an audience, Jade pointed to a couple of figurines on a wall shelf, as if she was talking about the display.

"I've been through this entire store. I checked the boxes under the counter," she hissed. "There's got to be more of these stupid goats somewhere."

"I don't know where Clyde kept everything," Randy insisted.

"What about your house?" Jade asked.

Randy looked at her, confused.

"Your mama told me you both lived with her."

Randy's face grew flush. He'd moved back in to look after his mother when his dad died and Clyde moved back after his divorce. Pauline had been there forever. Until this moment, he'd almost forgotten how embarrassing it all was.

"It's a temporary thing," he said. "Just helping out around the house. It's easier to just stay there."

"You need to get me to your house," Jade said. "Now."

Randy nodded, eagerly accepting the assignment. He then spoke loudly for everyone to hear.

"Thanks, baby," he said. "I never even noticed those before."

He turned to see Mama, Pauline and Sheriff McKinley all staring at them. He held up the goat figurine Jade had handed him.

"Defective merchandise," he offered in explanation. "A whole batch of 'em."

"I still want my ice cream," Pauline exclaimed.

"It's been a long day," Randy said, ignoring his aunt. "What do you say we all head home? Mama, is it okay if..."

He nodded toward Jade, hinting for an invitation.

"Are we just gonna stand here and pretend like we don't have a problem?" Mama replied.

Randy's heart sank.

"We all know Pauline is gonna be pissing and moaning about gawl dang ice cream until we get her some," Mama said. "And I'm not gonna deal with that all night."

"Damn right," Pauline agreed.

"How about we get her some ice cream on the way home?" Jade suggested. "My treat. And I mean it this time. Whatever anyone wants. It's the least I can do."

"That much is for damn sure," Mama snapped. "Come on. Me and Pauline will take my car. You done took Randall's car keys from him so you two gotta walk across the street like heathen folk."

Jade took the hit with a smile and Randy started corralling everyone out of the store.

"I'll see you ladies to your car," Sheriff McKinley offered.

As everyone single-filed it out the door, he stepped back, pulling a handkerchief from his pocket and discreetly picking up one of the figurines that Jade had been handling.

Mama turned around just as the sheriff shoved the figurine in his pocket.

"Why don't you come back to the house for a beer?" Mama asked.

Randy shot a panicked look to Jade, who silently motioned him to do something to prevent the intrusion.

"Oh, you probably have so much to do," Randy said. "You ain't got time for that."

"Nah, I'd be glad to stop by," the sheriff replied, never taking his eyes off of Jade, making it clear why he was accepting the offer.

The ragtag group filed out of The Lazy Goat, oblivious to the rusty brown Chevy pickup parked in the shadows at the back corner of the lot.

27

The two men in the truck watched the sheriff walk Mama and Pauline to their car while Randy and some woman locked the front door of the store.

"What the hell does that little bastard got going on?" Stonewall mumbled.

"And who's the hottie?" added Toby.

He shifted restlessly in his seat, rattling the empty beer cans on the floor and stirring up the stale cigarette smoke embedded deep in the seat fabric. Stonewall leaned forward on the steering wheel to better focus on the people leaving the store.

"Sheriff's there. I don't like the look of that."

Toby's attention was still on Jade.

"Man, she is sweeter than summer corn."

"She's a stranger," Stonewall reminded him. "And we don't trust strangers."

Stonewall had lived in Red Dirt his entire life. And other than beer runs and hunting trips, he never left it. He'd grown up poor. His dad had left before he even had any memories of him. His mother worked the night shift at the air conditioner factory in the neighboring town, which meant Stonewall was pretty much left to fend for himself. He had dropped out of school before reaching the sixth grade and eventually wound up running errands for a local bookie. Over the years, he had turned the gambling gig into a loan shark business. It was anything but lucrative, but it put food on Stonewall's plate and kept him out of factory work.

He never married and never claimed any kids. Toby was the son of his big sister and shared Stonewall's distaste for traditional work. Needing help and enjoying having someone look up to him, Stonewall had taken in his nephew. He wasn't the sharpest knife in the drawer, but he took orders well and, more importantly, he never questioned Stonewall.

They both watched as Randy and the mystery woman walked across the street to Perty's. That's when Stonewall noticed Randy's truck parked in front of the restaurant.

"Now why would he park over there?" he asked himself.

"So he wouldn't have to walk back after he ate?" Toby guessed.

Stonewall ignored his nephew and turned the key in the ignition. The old truck sputtered and coughed to life.

"Something's going on, that's for damn sure," he grumbled. "If that son of a bitch is trying to squirrel his way out of his debt, he's gonna walk into a world of hurt."

"What are we gonna do?" Toby asked.

Stonewall sneered.

"Maybe Randy don't know enough to be afraid of us. I think it's high time he found out."

"You already threatened him good."

"We've been too nice," Stonewall replied. "Sometimes if you wanna get shit done, you gotta tip over the outhouse."

28

They had barely pulled out of The Lazy Goat parking lot when Jade lit into Randy.

"What the hell is going on?" she demanded. "Why is the sheriff following us?"

"I didn't invite him!" Randy protested.

"You sure didn't do anything to stop it."

"Have you met my Mama? You don't stop things she starts."

"I know a way to stop all of this."

She pulled her gun out from her ankle holster and wiped it clean. Randy glanced down at it but pretended to play it cool.

"So you're just gonna shoot us now? That's how you solve problems?"

Jade pointed the gun at Randy.

"YOU are my problem. YOUR FAMILY is my problem. THAT SHERIFF is my problem. And this would certainly take care of all of you."

"Yeah, but then you got three dead bodies and still no goat."

"At least I'd have some peace and quiet," Jade muttered.

But she knew he was right. Like it or not, she needed his help. Hopefully, she would find the figurine at the house, but if not, she'd need him to figure out other possibilities. And Donovan had made it clear he didn't want any dead bodies if it could be helped.

The Philpot house was located just outside of town, off a county road and down a narrow red dirt path. It had grown dark since they had left The Lonely Goat and Randy's truck's headlights pierced the dark woods, lighting up swarms of flies and mosquitos.

Jade jostled side to side as the truck plodded over the rough road. Whenever they would hit a particularly large bump, the truck's suspension would creak loudly and they would both bounce in their seats.

Still, she thought. *It could be a long time before three bodies were found out here.*

She glanced at the side mirror to watch the headlights behind her. Mama was following first in her old red Cutlass Supreme. The sheriff's patrol car followed behind her.

"You need to get rid of the sheriff," she said. "Right away. You said you wanted to help. That's your way to help."

"How am I supposed to do that?"

"Figure it out. Your mother's life is in your hands."

As Randy felt the pressure of Jade's threat, the house appeared in the headlights. It was a modest ranch house with dark red wood siding and black shudders on either side of the windows. A fresh coat of paint seemed to cover most of the front of the house, but the portion that was unfinished revealed chipped, faded siding covered in mold and rot. Clearly, some renovations were taking place.

Randy parked the truck out in the clearing in front of the house. Mama's car pulled up next and the sheriff pulled up next to them. While everyone was getting out of their respective vehicles, Randy beelined it to the sheriff's car to catch him.

"Sheriff, you did not have to follow us all the way out here," Randy said.

The sheriff shot a confused look to Randy. "Well, your mama had asked if I could..."

"I know. But it's actually getting late for my mama," he said, clearly rescinding her offer.

Mama had overheard the conversation and butted in.

"It'd be alright if he stayed for one beer," she offered.

"He's on duty, Mama," Randy replied.

Sheriff McKinley smiled. He glanced at Jade and then back to Randy.

"I get it. You're probably done with company for the night," he said with a sly wink.

Randy smiled, happy to take the excuse.

"The sooner I can get Mama to bed the better, if you know what I mean," he said.

"I'll take a raincheck on that beer, Lucy," the sheriff said before turning his eyes toward Jade. "And sorry I startled you earlier, ma'am. Just doing my job."

The suspicious look in his eyes made it clear to Jade that he was still doing his job. But she played innocent and smiled back.

"I'm sorry, too," she said. "I hope you're not sore tomorrow."

Sheriff McKinley grinned and turned the patrol car around. As Randy watched the red taillights slowly disappear from view, Jade walked up next to him.

"Good job," she said.

Randy smiled. He felt a sense of pride. And relief. She squeezed his arm in what he assumed was a staged display of affection. Or was it sincere? Before he could really enjoy it, Mama stepped over and swung a big arm around Jade's shoulder, pulling her away and toward the house.

"Come on now. Let's get a bed ready for you."

Mama turned back to Randy and wagged a finger in his face.

"And, no, she will not be sleeping in your room. So you can just put those thoughts right out of your head."

"I got room in my bed!" Pauline offered. A little too enthusiastically.

"I don't want to put anyone out," Jade said sweetly. "Didn't Clyde have a room? I could just take that one."

"That is absolutely out of the question." Mama said, shaking her head.

"I just figured, since it's empty..."

"I don't know how you city folk do it in Dallas, but we have a sense of propriety here," Mama said. "How would that look? Us lending out his room before we even buried him?"

Jade nodded. So much for the easy way. She'd just have to wait until everyone fell asleep and then sneak into Clyde's room. Hopefully everyone would go to sleep quickly. If not, she might have to resort to Plan B.

29

Viktor Petrov nodded in appreciation as he took the glass of champagne from the flight attendant. He leaned back in his wide seat, took a sip and closed his eyes. His seat was in its own private cubicle, with a private television screen and self-serve refreshment area. It was separated from the seat next to it by a four-foot-high privacy wall with a sliding panel that Viktor chose to keep shut. While the plane had no first class section, Aeroflot's international business class rivaled the first class sections of many airlines. Cocooned inside four low walls with one open entryway, the seat afforded Viktor privacy.

Peter and Leo sat two rows back in adjoining seat/compartments. They chose to keep the sliding panel between their seats open. Peter had settled in to an in-flight movie. An American romantic comedy with an unrealistically beautiful cast. While he had never visited the United States before, he had met many Americans. And most of them were overweight and nothing like the people in this movie.

Leo leaned into the open area between their seats and motioned for Peter to take his headphones off.

"Do you know why the Texas is larger than Europe countries?" Leo said in broken English, reading from a magazine.

"Why are you talking in English?" Peter asked in Russian.

"Practice," Leo replied. "You should also practice, brother."

Peter nodded.

"So do you know?" Leo asked again.

"Russia is more big than Texas," Peter replied in English.

"Russia not count," Leo countered. "It is in Europe and Asia."

"So it is bigger," Peter repeated.

Leo gave up on the argument and returned to his magazine. "I want to buy cowboy hat."

Peter nodded, putting his headphones back on.

"Get boots," Peter said. "You can wear them more when we return. Wearing cowboy hat in Russia will make you look like fool."

"How long to be in Texas?" Leo asked.

Peter sighed and removed his headphones again.

"One day. Two."

"Maybe we stay longer," Leo suggested. "Take in sights. See The Alamo."

"Nyet. The sooner we get back, the better," Peter said. "In America, we are not...how do they say...under the radar. The FBI will not look away. They are probably already following."

Leo looked around at the other seat compartments. The walls hid the identities of the other business class passengers, but he could tell it was a full flight.

"On plane? Now?"

Peter shrugged. But then he noted the fear in his brother's eyes and smiled.

"Relax, brother," he said. "We have plans in place once we get to Texas. They will not find us."

30

J ade lay on her half of the saggy bed, staring at the
ceiling as Pauline snored loudly beside her. Luckily,
everyone had gone to bed very quickly. It was now a
matter of waiting long enough for everyone to fall into
a deep enough sleep before she could start her hunt. Feeling
confident she was the only one awake, she slipped quietly out
of the bed. Mama had given her an old Dallas Cowboys T-shirt
to sleep in, but Jade had opted to stay dressed for a quicker
midnight getaway. Pauline had thought it was foolish.

"You gotta let your lady parts breathe at night," she had
said.

Jade had told her she was shy around strangers and would
sleep better in her clothes. It was enough to pacify Pauline,
although she had insisted her guest remove her shoes.

Jade grabbed her shoes and tip-toed out of the room, the
wooden floor creaking under every step. She walked lightly and
slowly down the hall to the door of Clyde's room. Mama had
helpfully pointed it out, although she had done so warning that
everyone was forbidden to go inside.

She opened the door slowly, relieved when it didn't creak.

Using the flashlight on her phone, she looked around and was shocked by what she saw. The room was in shambles. If Jade didn't know any better, she would have guessed that someone had beat her to it and had already torn the place apart. But who would have done that? Most likely, the mess was just the way Clyde lived.

Resigning herself to a long night, she began methodically going through every inch of the room. The dirty clothes thrown everywhere. The stacks of porn and hunting magazines piled in a corner. The closet filled with hunting gear, record albums, and shoeboxes of animal bones. She checked for hidden compartments in the floor and under the bed. Her heart began to race at one point when she found a small black safe with a combination lock. The lock posed no problem, and she was able to open it in less than a minute, only to find several hundred dollars, a passport and some nude Polaroids of a somewhat younger Amy Jo.

After a couple of hours, Jade began to lose hope. She had scoured every inch of the room and found nothing.

Where else would Clyde hide a valuable contraband?

She looked out the window and noticed something she hadn't seen before. She stepped closer to get a better angle. Outside, the full moon cast a blue-white glow through the woods. It landed on a canopy of ivy which, through the shadows, Jade could barely make out an old gray wooden shed.

31

J ade easily yanked the rusted padlock away and opened the weathered door of the shed. A moldy, earthy smell rushed to escape the confines and Jade flinched at the odor. Using a flashlight she had found in Clyde's bedroom, she surveyed the interior of the shed, which was crammed full of long-forgotten junk. In addition to the rusted lawn equipment and engine parts, there were also half-decayed cardboard boxes and black plastic yard bags full of old clothes and toys.

It looked like no one had stepped foot in the shed for decades, but without other options, Jade resigned herself to digging through the rubble anyway. She positioned the flashlight in a corner to help illuminate the room and quietly pulled down one of the plastic bags. Before she could open it, she was interrupted by a familiar voice.

"You're even braver than I thought if you're touching anything in this rat trap," Randy said.

Jade spun around, instinctively drawing her gun and pointing it at him.

Randy raised his hands in surrender, holding a bottle of Jack Daniel's in one of them. From the way he swayed side by side, it was pretty clear he had already been drinking.

"Any luck?" Randy asked, trying to hide a slight slur in his speech.

"Nothing in his room," Jade replied. "You're just in time to help me with all of this."

"How'd you even get in?" Randy asked. "This thing has been locked for years and we lost the key."

"Did you ever try just pulling on it?" Jade asked.

Randy looked at the spot on the door where the lock had been pulled from the rotting wood.

"Never thought of that," he muttered. "But if that lock was still on the door when you got here, it means Clyde didn't think of it either."

"Maybe he had a key and didn't tell anyone," Jade suggested.

But, before he could reply, she decided to quickly check her own theory. She found the lock laying in the grass and examined the key slot. It was so rusted out she could tell right away it hadn't been used in years. She threw it back on the ground.

"Where else would he have hid something?" Jade asked.

Randy shrugged. "I don't know."

Jade stepped up to Randy, looking him square in the eyes. "Think. Hard."

Randy squinted, trying to force his liquored brain to focus. Coming up empty-handed, he shook his head.

"I swear. I have no idea."

Jade sighed.

"It's gotta be in the shop. I'm taking your truck back," she said, walking past him.

"Oh, I don't let people drive my truck," Randy said, too drunk to think about what he was saying and to whom he was saying it.

But the way Jade glared hard at him immediately reminded him that she was calling all the shots. Still, he was relaxed enough to not be completely intimidated.

"Fine. Take it. But at least share a drink first," he said, waving the whiskey bottle.

Jade grabbed the bottle from his hand and threw back a large swallow.

"Well, that was fun," she said sarcastically, handing the bottle back. "Hate to run, but there's work to be done."

She pulled the keys from her pocket. She had grabbed them off of the kitchen counter earlier, along with Mama's keys, to ensure no one would be able to make a break for it.

"That was having a drink," Randy said, missing the sarcasm. "I asked you to share a drink."

He grabbed the keys from her hand before she even realized what had happened and stumbled his way toward an old yellow couch sitting next to a rusted-out steel drum which seemed to be used for fires.

"Come on," he said. "The store ain't going nowhere."

In any other circumstance, she would have shot him in the back of the head without even thinking about it. But something made her stop. He clearly posed no real threat. And he was right. The store wasn't going anywhere. Donovan had texted her an update on Viktor Petrov's pending arrival and the earliest he could get to Red Dirt would be late afternoon. Besides, if she was completely honest with herself, she could use another drink.

Randy plopped down on the faded yellow couch. It was covered in water stains, cigarette burns and God knows what else.

"You're taking my truck. Destroying my brother's store. Everyone's gonna know you ain't my girlfriend and I'm gonna be the laughingstock of the entire town on the day of my brother's funeral. And all that's if you don't kill me. Least you can do is share a drink with me first."

Jade shook her head and put the gun away, nudging Randy to move over and give her room to sit.

32

Randy and Jade passed the whiskey bottle back and forth. Randy, already a quarter of a bottle ahead of her, slouched on the couch and leaned his head back, closing his eyes. Jade sat forward and stared straight ahead into nothing as she retraced her steps, trying to think about where else Clyde could have hid the stupid figurine.

"This is nice, ain't it?" Randy sighed.

He opened an eye to get a peek at Jade's intense concentration.

"Well, I like it," he said, answering his own question.

A chorus of crickets and tree frogs created a steady, one-note melody that filled the air, punctuated by the occasional bass note of a distant bullfrog.

"Hear that?" Randy asked again.

"Frogs and crickets," Jade replied.

"If you wanna get technical," Randy laughed. "To me, it's what nighttime sounds like. Ain't it relaxing? Kinda like a cat purring. Know what I mean?"

Jade broke her concentration long enough to look at Randy.

"You're drunk."

His eyes still shut, he smiled in agreement. Jade studied him. Here was this good ol' boy sitting beside his captor, someone who had repeatedly threatened his life and that of his family, and he was smiling drunk and talking about crickets purring like cats.

He's either dumb as rocks or Zen as a Buddhist monk, she thought.

She decided to give her mind a break and let her subconscious do the work for a bit. And when she leaned back and took in a deep inhale of the country air, she realized it was the first time she had taken a moment to relax since, well, she couldn't even remember the last time.

"So where are you from?" Randy asked.

Jade put her finger to her lips. "Shhh. I'm listening to the cats purr."

Randy grinned, but her lack of an answer only piqued his interest.

"How'd you get into this line of work anyway?" he asked. "Did you apply for it? Answer a want ad? Just fall into it? Is it a family business?"

Jade shook her head. "I have no family."

"Bullshit. Everybody's got family."

"Who was that girl in the picture you were looking at?" Jade asked, changing the subject.

"Huh?" Randy stammered, clearly thrown by the question. "What picture?"

"When I met you. You were sitting in your truck looking a picture. Is that your ex-girlfriend?"

Randy sighed and nodded.

"I try to forget about her, but then these reminders pop up out of nowhere and sabotage me."

"So, it was serious?"

Randy nodded his head.

"I thought so. I thought she was the one. Thought she felt the same. Guess I was wrong about that."

Jade immediately regretted bring up the subject and tried to think of a new topic. But she had let the genie out of the bottle.

"Things were fine and then one day out of the blue she wants to break up," he continued. "Tells me it wasn't 'me.' She just needed to be alone for a while."

He laughed to himself.

"Couple of months later, I find out she's dating this rich, ex-jock from high school."

"Ouch," was all Jade could muster.

Things had gotten way too personal way too fast for her liking. But Randy went on, oblivious to Jade's discomfort.

"You ever gone from thinking you're the most important person in someone's life to knowing you don't even matter? To go from being their one true love—their soulmate—and then see how easy they replace you? It a kick in the nuts."

Jade looked at Randy and saw tears welling up in his eyes. Realizing she was looking, he quickly pushed the tears back.

"I know what you're gonna say," he went on. "It's her loss. Someday she'll realize her mistake. Blah blah blah."

"No. She probably won't," Jade replied matter-of-factly.

Randy was slightly stunned by the dose of tough love.

"But who gives a shit? She moved on so you've got to move on. And to be honest, sounds like you dodged a bullet."

Randy snickered and puffed himself up with a moment of self-confidence.

"I treated her real good, you know. I was there for her through all kinds of shit. And then she throws me out like a bag of trash? I deserved better."

Jade shrugged.

"Who cares what you 'deserved'? She obviously doesn't," Jade said. "Deserved has got nothing to do with it. People don't always get what they deserve–good or bad. There's no justice to it. There's no karma. Life's a bitch and at some point she's gonna stab you in the back."

"Well, you're a ray of sunshine," Randy replied.

"You've just got to get out of your head," Jade said. "Get a change of scenery. Go somewhere. Do something different. I bet you've lived right here your whole life."

Randy shrugged. "I lived in Austin during college."

Jade looked at Randy in shock.

"You went to college?"

"Is that so surprising?" he asked with a smirk.

He passed the bottle to Jade, who took a small sip. She couldn't afford to get drunk. There was still too much to do.

"So, Austin, huh? What were you in for?" Jade asked.

Randy hesitated before answering.

"I was gonna be an optometrist."

Jade laughed out loud.

"Seriously? An eye doctor?"

"Why not? It's the perfect job," Randy replied, happy to change the subject. "Patients come to see you and you just make them look in machines that tell you all you need to know. If the patient needs glasses, you send 'em off over to the glasses person. If they have eye problems or need surgery, you send 'em to an opthalmologist. No muss, no fuss."

Jade shook her head. "I think there's a lot more to it than that."

Randy shrugged.

"It don't matter anyway."

"You flunk out?"

"I was on the honor roll, thank you very much."

"So, what happened?"

"Life," he answered. "Or death, really."

33

Agent Bennet squeezed his body tight to accommodate the two massive men spilling out of the seats on either side of him. After several hours of stand-by seats that didn't pan out, he was finally able to catch a flight out of Ronald Reagan Airport. The 737 was crammed with passengers and Dean had been able to wrestle the one empty seat left on the plane. Now wedged between two giants, Dean found his arms pinned helplessly to his side.

I should get my ticket half price for only getting half a seat, he grumbled, as he attempted to maneuver his arms enough to pull out the laptop he had stored in the seat pocket in front of him.

The Goliath in the window seat, engrossed in a romance novel, moved his arm to give Dean just enough room to grab the computer, only to drop it back down and pin the agent's arms again. Dean tried to slip his other arm free but, even though they had only been in the air ten minutes, the hulk in the aisle seat was already sound asleep.

But while his arms were pinned, he could still move his

wrists and hands and Dean struggled to eventually open his laptop, connect to a hotspot and check his email. His efforts were rewarded with a message from Agent Chin. Dean opened the attached excel spreadsheet.

Chin had somehow managed to get the shipping log for PJD, the American import company not so secretly run by Alex Petrov's organization. While the log didn't list contents of each shipment, it did include number of boxes and destination. Chin had already done Dean the favor of eliminating all shipments except those going to Texas or surrounding areas in the past two weeks.

Dean began to skim the list, looking for anything unusual. Most of the shipments included a large quantity of boxes. He was hoping to find an anomaly. Something like the single box sent priority to...

"The Lazy Goat?" Dean read aloud. "In Red Dirt, Texas."

This had to be the one. A single package sent five days ago to a remote location. Dean struggled to open a web browser to find the location of Red Dirt. As he waited for a map to download, he tried to catch the attention of a passing flight attendant by moving his head.

The attendant noticed him and, upon seeing his claustrophobic situation, gave him an apologetic smile.

"I'm so sorry about this," she said quietly.

"How much longer is the flight?" Dean asked.

The flight attendant winced at the question because she knew he wasn't going to like the answer.

"About three hours, sir," she said. "Can I get you anything to drink or something?"

Dean lifted his hands to illustrate what little mobility he had.

"Not unless you have really long straws," he joked with a smile.

The attendant nodded and offered to help anyway she could, knowing full well there was nothing she could do. Dean nodded and sighed in resignation as she walked away. It was enough to stir the sleeping giant beside him, who shifted his position and leaned in, resting his head on Dean's shoulder.

34

As the whiskey bottle got lighter, Randy and Jade had taken to sipping what was left so it would last longer.

"So, your dad died and you just gave up everything and came home?" Jade asked in disbelief.

"Didn't have a choice," he answered. "Mama was a mess and Clyde ain't never been good at doing much more than raising hell."

Jade started to say something but decided against it. Randy smiled.

"I'd already decided I was gonna quit anyway."

"Too much science?"

"Nah. Just not my thing."

He twirled the whiskey bottle in front of him to watch the brown liquid spin.

"So what is your thing?"

Randy shook his head.

"You'll laugh."

"Try me."

Randy looked at her, grinning that stupid boyish grin.

"I wanna be a boat captain. Run a deep-sea fishing charter."

"A boat captain?" Jade asked. "There's nothing wrong with that."

The topic energized Randy.

"I've got a buddy from college. His family has a charter business in Florida and his folks are retiring. He asked me to partner with him. I don't even need to invest anything. I can work off my share."

"Sounds like a dream to me," Jade said. "What are you still doing here?"

The energy rushed out of Randy like a deflating balloon.

"Mama," he said.

Jade laughed, but when she looked in his eyes, she realized he wasn't kidding.

"Oh, shit. You're serious."

"I can't just up and leave her. Especially now that Clyde's gone. I don't know if you noticed, but this house is falling apart."

"And it's your responsibility to fix it? Who says?" Jade asked. "That's bullshit. You've got one person to look out for in this life. Yourself."

"You don't understand," he said. "My Mama needs me."

"Trust me, your mother can take care of herself."

Randy shook his head, not buying it.

"She'd kill me."

"She'd be fine."

"Nothing personal, but you don't seem like the type of person who can be doling out life advice."

"You don't know anything about me," Jade replied.

"Not for lack of trying. I don't even know your name," he said. "I'm guessing it's not Jen."

Jade suddenly felt an urge to tell him everything. How she grew up all over the world, the child of a military family. How her father died when she was 13 and her mother disappeared in grief. How she struck out on her own as a teenager, resorting to petty theft and, because she was good at it, slowly turning to bigger crimes. How Donovan Fontaine discovered her when she had tried to rob his house, and recognizing her potential, took her in. He became a twisted father figure. A Fagin to her Artful Dodger. How she had worked so hard to hide her identity that she wasn't even sure if she had one anymore.

But instead, she smiled softly.

"I'm your internet girlfriend who is going to find what I'm looking for and then disappear. And you will never, ever tell anyone why I was here or what I was looking for or I will come back and kill you and your family."

"How romantic."

"No one has ever seen me and lived to tell the tale," she said. "I'm making a big exception here because, for some stupid reason, probably jet lag, I trust you. Don't make me regret it. I know where you live now."

Randy laughed nervously but Jade stared at him, unflinching, to make her point. His smile quickly faded away.

"Okay, okay," Randy said. "I get it. Nothing. Nada. Zilch. Zipped shut. Man, talk about your buzz kill."

He lifted the bottle to his lips and was disappointed to find it empty. He let it tumble to the ground.

"Welp, I guess happy hour is over," he groaned. "Just promise me you won't hurt my truck. She ain't much, but she's all I got."

Jade had almost forgot about driving back to the store. Maybe it was the whiskey or maybe the cool country air, but she felt some of the tightness in her back loosening and she wasn't sure she was quite ready to let it go.

She leaned back and looked up at the stars.

"I'll leave in a minute."

35

The steady, hypnotic nighttime chirping of crickets had been replaced with the busy chatter of morning birds. The sun crept above the distant tree line and obnoxiously directed its golden morning rays on the yellow couch.

Randy snored gently, his head resting on Jade's shoulder. She slept peacefully into him as well. But they were both yanked out of their slumber when Mama kicked Randy in the shin.

"What the hell are you doing?" she bellowed.

The pair both bolted up, surprised at how close they were to each other. Mama stood over them, wearing a light blue housecoat and sporting giant rollers in her hair.

Randy grabbed his shin. "Dang it, Mama!"

Jade, who wasn't used to being caught off guard, immediately checked to make sure her gun was still strapped into her ankle holster.

"I don't know this one from Adam," the large woman yelled, pointing at Jade. "But I raised you better than this."

"I didn't do anything," Randy protested, rubbing his temples. "I mean, I don't think..."

Jade's incredulous glare quickly confirmed that nothing had happened.

"We were just talking and fell asleep," he explained.

"Well, now you're burning daylight and I got breakfast cooking," Mama replied, still yelling. "Today is your brother's funeral and we got a lot to do. Did you get his suit over to the funeral home? And his shoes?"

"What's he need shoes for?" Randy asked.

"I don't know," Mama snapped. "What does he need a suit for?"

As soon as they started talking about the funeral, Jade's mind started whirring back to life.

Of course, she thought. *Why didn't I think of it earlier?*

"It's alright, Mama. Just calm down," Randy said, standing quickly. He immediately regretted it and had to reach behind him to steady himself on the couch arm.

"Don't you tell me to calm down," she said, poking her son in the chest.

He wasn't stable enough to keep his balance and fell back to a sitting position on the couch again

"I'm burying my son today," Mama yelled. "I will get as riled up as I damn well please. And why are you sitting down again? Get up and help me!"

Randy stood again, looking back at Jade, who was clearly plotting something.

"Lucas is helping me," Randy said quietly, trying to calm his mother. "He's the funeral director so I think he knows what he's doing. You ain't gotta worry about nothing. I've got it under control."

Suddenly, Mama's eyes lit up.

"The gawl-darned bacon is burning!"

She turned in a half-run to the house, yelling as she went.

"Pauline, save the bacon!"

Jade stood up.

"Take me to the funeral home," she said.

"I'm going right after breakfast," Randy explained.

"Now," Jade insisted.

Randy nodded, sensing the urgency in Jade's voice.

"Can I ask why?" Randy asked, already afraid of the answer.

"I can't believe I didn't think of it," Jade answered.

"Think of what?"

Jade ignored the question and beelined it to the truck. Randy struggled to follow, clearly still feeling the effects of the alcohol.

"Did you get his belongings already?" she asked. "After he died?"

"They gave me all his things," Randy said, slowly catching up to Jade's thinking. "There weren't no goats."

"Maybe it wasn't ON him," Jade replied.

Randy froze, worrying that didn't mean what he thought it meant.

"Let's go," Jade yelled, sliding into the truck behind the steering wheel.

Randy walked to the passenger side of his truck, something he had never done before. He yelled out to his mother as he got in.

"Mama, we're gonna go see Lucas now," he yelled, the sound of his own voice punctuating his head like a pickaxe.

The truck engine roared and, before Randy could completely shut his door, Jade took off. As they turned and sped down the path, Mama emerged from the house, spatula in hand.

"Randy! Get your butt back here right now!" she yelled.

She fumed as she watched them speed away then spun around and stormed back into the house.

"The boy gets a whiff of female and his brain shuts plum

off," she muttered to herself. "Well, I ain't gonna let him ruin things."

She slipped her hand into her housecoat's pocket.

"I got my good luck charm and it's all gonna be okay."

She pulled the small plastic goat figurine from her pocket and kissed it gently, before storming back into the house.

36

D ean pulled the rented Ford Taurus on to Interstate 35 away from DFW International Airport. Even though it was the cheapest car available from the rental agency, it was newer - and light years better - than Dean's own car. It had taken him awhile to figure out how to sync up the car's GPS with his phone but now he was headed east toward Red Dirt with an arrival time of approximately 10:30 a.m.

It should have been a lot earlier. Dean's flight had landed on time the night before but had then taxied on the tarmac for over an hour. He had heard about DFW's reputation for long taxiing times, a regrettable by-product of being such a large airport. But severe weather up the West Coast had created a rash of delayed flights... and unavailable gates.

It had taken him nearly a half hour to reach the car rental agency. It had taken nearly that long for him to get the feeling back in both of his arms after his crammed flight. He couldn't help but think of the classic joke, I've been flying all night... and, boy, are my arms tired.

The car rental agency was another travesty. They had misplaced his reservation and were having a hard time finding a replacement. After about thirty minutes that seemed like two hours, they sent him to a different rental agency where he was able to grab the last car available. In the end, it had cost him an extra three hours of time he did not have.

The Dallas skyline loomed in front of him, as did a sea of red taillights.

Great. I hit Dallas right at peak rush hour.

The GPS offered no alternative routes. All he could do was sit it out and drink the lukewarm coffee he had picked up at the airport.

He had thought about contacting the local FBI office to alert them of his mission but decided against it. For one, he was technically on vacation and if Strickland found out what he was doing, he'd send a team to pull him out before he even reached Red Dirt. This was definitely a case of it being better to ask for forgiveness rather than permission. Besides, the agency was sure to have a tail on Viktor Petrov, so they would all wind up at the same place anyway. Better for the agency to put their resources toward the Russian mob boss and not the rumor of a thief.

The thief.

He wondered if Jade was still in Red Dirt or if she'd already found her contraband and slipped back out. That would be her standard M.O. However, Dean had checked police reports in the area and there had been no reports of unusual robberies. Or murders.

But why would she still be there? Could he have the wrong location?

Dean began to question his investigative work. And as soon as he let doubt creep into his brain, he began second-guessing everything. He began to think about what he would do if he actually did find her. She wasn't likely to surrender quietly. Dean hadn't fired a weapon in the line of duty. Ever. She clearly had the upper hand if a confrontation occurred. Plus, there were the civilians to consider. She wouldn't hesitate to use any one of them as a human shield. Was he putting innocent people in harm's way just so he could play Lone Ranger?

On the other hand, he rationalized, he had the element of surprise on his side. She was most likely expecting Viktor Petrov to show up and would even expect the FBI to follow him. But she wouldn't be looking for a lone agent coming in first. Of course, that's because it would be a suicide mission.

Dean had been so caught up in catching Jade that he had never thought about the very real possibility he may not come out of this alive. And now that he did, he was surprised he didn't really care. It's not like he had a death wish or was suicidal, but it's not like he had a lot to lose. He had no one. He had nothing of value. He had nothing really worth living for. And, truth be told, this crazy pursuit of a mysterious and dangerous international thief had woken him up a little bit. In fact, he hadn't felt this alive in years.

37

R andy's truck screeched to a halt in the empty parking lot of the East Pines Funeral Home. Jade jumped out and hurried toward the door. Randy climbed out of the passenger seat, moving much slower.

"I should have done this first thing," Jade said to herself.

"You shouldn't have done it at all," Randy argued. "You still shouldn't."

"It's just a pile of sticks and meat," she replied.

Randy maneuvered himself in front of Jade, blocking the door.

"That pile of sticks and meat is my brother," he protested.

"I promise. He won't feel a thing."

She pushed him aside and jiggled the doorknob. It was locked. Randy sighed, resigning himself to the fact he didn't really have a choice in the matter, and reached up, feeling along the top rim of the doorsill until he found the key.

Jade stormed down the hallway, leaving Randy in her tracks. On the ride over, she had pulled her gun from the ankle holster and tucked it into the back waist of her jeans. He noticed the gun as he watched her turn into a room, but when he saw the sign over the door that read EMBALMING, he hesitated. But feeling a family duty to protect the sanctity of his brother, he took a deep breath and pushed the swinging door open.

The room was small. Bright fluorescent lights reflected off of the white tile floors, causing Randy to squint. His gaze quickly planted on two gurneys sitting side by side in the middle of the room, both were draped in white sheets that were clearly covering bodies.

"I don't think we should be in here," Randy said, turning away only to find a casket sitting on another gurney. He caught his breath and turned back around just as Jade yanked one of the sheets back. It was an elderly woman with gray-white skin and blue lips.

Randy gasped in recognition.

"Mrs. Humphrey?" he said. "I didn't even know she was sick!"

He studied the dead woman as Jade walked over to the other gurney.

"I mean, she was like a million years old," Randy continued. "But I just figured she was never gonna die."

He tenderly pulled the sheet back over her head and looked up just as Jade yanked the sheet away from the other body. He walked over in silence, staring at the familiar face.

"That him?" Jade asked.

Randy stared at the body, not sure what to think.

"I don't know," Randy muttered.

"You don't know?" Jade asked.

A wave of recognition and relief washed over Randy.

"Thank God," he said "That's Johnny Bemus. I think, anyways. I ain't seen him in maybe five years and he didn't have a beard then. Jeez, what coulda happened to him? I didn't even know he was still around."

"But it's not Clyde?" Jade interrupted.

"Definitely not Clyde."

They both looked at the casket but were interrupted by the sound of someone approaching the door. Before either could react, a portly man with round-rimmed glasses casually pushed open the door, a cup of coffee in one hand and a donut in the other. He had just taken a big bite out of the pastry and froze mid-chew when he saw the two intruders staring back at him in shock.

38

L ucas Shaver didn't move. He did, however, manage to swallow the chunk of donut in his mouth.

"What the holy hell?" he said.

Randy noticed Jade instinctively reach around her back and put her hand on her gun. Knowing he needed to quickly diffuse the situation, he turned to Lucas and smiled.

"Hey, buddy," Randy said. "Sorry to startle you. I stopped by to see if there's anything I need to do before the funeral."

"How did you... what are you... you can't be in here."

Switching on her Texas personality, Jade grinned ear to ear and walked over to Randy's side.

"This is all my fault," she twanged. "I'm so sorry."

Lucas looked at her, confused.

"And who are..."

"Oh, I'm Jen Brown. Randy's girlfriend."

Lucas looked at Jade then at Randy, who nodded in agreement. His shocked expression turned to one of surprise and finally relief.

"Holy hell. You got yourself a new girlfriend, Randy?" he said. "Why didn't you tell me?"

"Randy's been grieving so I thought we should come take a look at his brother in private," Jade went on. "You know, before everyone else."

Lucas looked at Randy who, playing along with Jade's story, overacted being sad and pretended to cry.

"It hit me harder than I thought it would," Randy said through fake tears.

Randy looked at Jade for approval and was surprised to see her slightly shaking her head in discreet disapproval.

"You know we offer private viewings before the service, Randy," Lucas said.

"Yeah, but his mama is gonna want all of that," Jade rationalized. "And you know Mama."

Lucas nodded. He knew all too well. He had dealt with many grieving mothers in the course of his fifteen-year career, but none of them had micromanaged and even bullied at the level of Randy's mama. In fact, Lucas was a nervous wreck at the thought of having to deal with her today.

"I totally understand," he said. "You need to be able to grieve on your own so you'll be strong enough to be there for your mother later."

Randy nodded, toning down the tears.

"I shoulda called but I didn't wanna bother you," he said.

Lucas pointed to the wall of what looked like storage lockers.

"He's still chilling in there. Almost ready for his big day," Lucas said. "I got these other bodies out for embalming and then went and grabbed some breakfast."

He stopped before opening one of the doors to a refrigerator chamber.

"I'm not quite done with him. I do the final touches after I dress him."

"Is he... disfigured? On account of the way he died?" Randy asked in horror.

Lucas laughed and shook his head.

"Oh, Lord no. The accident only messed him up down there," Lucas answered, pointing to his crotch. "But the prime viewing area was unscathed. I just need to add a little color to his face. Comb his hair. Stuff like that."

Randy smiled.

"I can't even remember the last time I saw Clyde's hair combed."

"Do you have his shoes?" Lucas asked. "Your mama said you were gonna bring them over this morning."

Randy started to ask the mortician why his brother would need shoes in a casket, but Jade stepped in front of him.

"Change of plans. No shoes," she said. "But do you think Randy could have a moment alone with his brother?"

Lucas seemed worried. "But Mama specifically said..."

"We convinced her heaven feels better on bare feet and if he goes south they're just gonna melt to his feet," Jade explained. "About Randy?"

Lucas nodded then turned to Randy.

"Of course," he said. "Just don't touch him, please."

39

L ucas opened the refrigerator door and slid the gurney out, pulling back the sheet enough to reveal Clyde's head and chest. Randy let out a small gasp at the sight of his brother's body. His skin was the same white gray as the other bodies and his cheeks seemed sunk in. It looked LIKE Clyde, but NOT Clyde. Almost like a wax figure of his brother. Also, his medium length brown hair was poofed up like a troll doll. Randy slowly stepped closer. He had been the one to identify his brother's body after the accident but, for some reason, this felt more real. And an unexpected wave of grief swept over Randy.

Lucas stepped back next to Jade.

"Do you think we could be alone with him?" Jade whispered. "For just a few minutes?"

Lucas hesitated but, after looking into Jade's big pleading eyes, he nodded.

"I'll be back in a few," he said. "Just please don't touch anything."

Jade nodded and watched as Lucas walked out the door. As

soon as it shut, she shifted back to being all business, completely ignoring Randy's now-fragile state.

"Okay. I'm going to need you to help me turn him over."

She started to move the body but realized Randy was making no effort to help. She looked up to see him staring down at the body, his eyes filled with tears. Jade sighed and looked nervously toward the door.

"I'm sorry, Randy," she offered as gently as her sense of urgency allowed.

Randy could barely muster a nod.

"I was never really close with him," he replied, his voice quivering.

Jade took a deep breath. She needed to be patient, but Randy's grieving process was on a tight deadline.

"But I always looked up to him in a weird way," Randy went on. "The way he just did what he wanted. I always wanted to be more like that."

"Yeah, well you're alive and he isn't," Jade reminded him. "Being a free spirit has a price."

"I couldn't be one. I always had to clean up his mess. And it pissed me off how much Mama loved him anyway," Randy went on. "All he did was give her grief. Everything he did broke her heart. And she just loved him harder."

Jade awkwardly patted Randy on the shoulder, hoping the condolence would help move things along.

"I want to hate him," Randy said. "But, gawl-dangit, I just can't. He's my brother."

Randy wiped real tears from his eyes and tried to collect himself.

"I like to think that the last thing he felt was the relief of having to finally take a piss, and not the shock that came after," Randy said. "That relief is such a good feeling."

Jade nodded, not sure how to respond.

"Yes, it is," she found herself saying. "I'm sure that's what he felt."

Jade put her comforting arms around Randy and pulled him away from Clyde's body. She realized he was going to be of no use to her and it would probably be better for everyone if she did this alone.

"Randy, why don't you go wait in the truck?" she gently suggested.

Randy nodded, sniffling back his tears.

"You're not gonna cut him open or anything or you?" Randy asked.

Jade found a box of latex gloves near the gurneys.

"I wish it were that easy," she said as she snapped one on her right hand.

40

The commercial produce truck backed up to the warehouse loading dock where three men were waiting. As soon as the truck pulled to a stop, one of the men lifted its rear door and peered into the darkness. He took a step back as Leo and Peter Koslov emerged from the truck, followed by Viktor Petrov.

While Leo and Peter spoke to the men in Russian, Viktor headed toward an elderly man who was leaning back against a pallet of boxes.

"Are you sure we were not followed?" Viktor asked in Russian.

The elderly man grinned.

"You can't ever be sure of nothing," he said in a Texas accent. "But the FBI is hot on the trail of our decoy and headed far away from here."

Anticipating FBI presence upon his arrival, Viktor had contacted a Texas outfit to arrange a diversion. Upon departing the plane, Viktor, Peter and Leo had ducked into a men's room, fully aware they were being followed. Once in the men's room, they each went into stalls and waited. After a few minutes, three men dressed identical to Viktor, Leo and Peter emerged from the bathroom and headed out of the airport.

While the FBI followed the look-alikes, Viktor and the twins were met by a janitor, who escorted them through an employee door down a long corridor that eventually led to the loading docks. The three Russians climbed into the back of a produce truck, where they waited an extra thirty minutes. Finally, the truck left the airport and took a convoluted route to a railyard warehouse located 25 miles west of the airport.

Meanwhile, the FBI followed the decoy Russians to a black Lincoln town car which headed south to Waco. By the time the FBI would figure out they were following the wrong trio, Viktor Petrov would be well on his way to Red Dirt.

The grinning man was Jimmy Craddock, an old Texan opportunist whose greed saw no borders. He had been working with the Petrov crime syndicate way before Viktor rose to the top of the ranks. In fact, it was Jimmy that had introduced the Petrovs to Clyde Philpot, a down-on-his-luck gambler who owed Jimmy a lot of money and would be more than willing to help smuggle stolen goods in and out of the country.

"I got you a truck over here," Jimmy said, motioning to another loading dock.

"A truck?" Viktor asked in broken English. "I asked for sedan."

"Well, if you wanna stick out like a sore thumb, I can arrange for one," Jimmy replied. "But if you want to drive out of here without raising any eyebrows, I suggest you take a Texas carriage."

The two men walked toward the other loading dock, followed by Leo and Peter, who had been given American currency, burner phones, firearms and ammunition. They all reached the black Ford F-150 pickup truck at the same time. It was spacious, had a rear seat, and sat so tall it had a built-in step to help you climb inside.

"Yes!" Leo exclaimed, jumping in the back of the truck. "Real Texas truck!"

Peter walked beside Viktor as both men studied the large vehicle.

"It seems big," Peter offered. "I am sure it has comfort."

Jimmy handed the keys to Viktor who handed them to Peter without saying a word.

"Let us hope," Viktor grumbled, walking around the truck.

"Shotgun!" an exuberant Leo yelled out as he lept out of the back of the pickup and opened the front passenger door.

Viktor shot him a glare that immediately reminded him this was not a joyride. Leo wiped the smile off of his face and stood to aside.

"I will ride in backseat," Leo said quietly as Viktor climbed into the truck.

andy sat behind the wheel of his truck, staring blindly at the funeral home in front of him. He was stunned that seeing his brother's body affected him as much as it did. Like he had said, they weren't that close, and, if he was truly honest with himself, life would have been much easier if he wasn't always having to clean up his brother's messes.

He thought about the woman inside the funeral home performing some sort of morbid cavity search on his dead brother.

What am I doing? he thought. *What am I getting myself caught up in?*

He could get away right now. Granted, she still had his truck keys, but he could make it to the sheriff's station on foot. Or he could even go inside and ask for Lucas's help. This was his chance.

But he knew he wasn't going to take it. Not because he was afraid, but because he didn't want to. Truth be told, he was actually enjoying this treasure hunt. And he was enjoying her company. But none of it mattered. If she found what she was looking for on Clyde – or rather, in Clyde – she'd be on her way and out of his life in less than an hour. He'd bury his brother, console his mother and life would return to its same boring, everyday pattern, with its same old set of problems.

As if on cue, the approaching clatter of an old engine caught his attention and he looked up to see Stonewall's rusty truck pulling into the parking lot. It came to a stop right behind Randy's truck, effectively pinning him in.

"Shit balls," Randy growled as Stonewall and Toby climbed out of their truck.

He locked the driver's side door and quickly reached across to lock the passenger door. Unfortunately, Toby was quicker. He flung the door open, sliding into the seat.

"Hey, Randy," Toby said. "Whatcha doing?"

Stonewall tapped on the driver's side window and motioned for Randy to step out of the truck. Knowing he was trapped, Randy let out a sigh and opened the door. As he climbed out of the truck, Toby scootched across the seat to get out behind him. Stonewall grabbed Randy by the shirt collar and pinned him against the truck. Randy flinched as Stonewall leaned in close. His rancid breath smelled like cigarettes and old beer stuffed inside a dead possum.

"You think I'm a total fool?" he snarled.

When he didn't answer, Toby answered for him. "I think he does."

"I told you I'd get you the money," Randy said. "It ain't even been 24 hours."

"I know you're up to something," Stonewall accused, shaking a pointed finger in Randy's face.

Randy shook off Stonewall's grip.

"I don't know what you're talking about," Randy said.

"That girl you're hanging around with," Stonewall said, trying to bait him.

"Good looking girl, too," Toby added, much to Stonewall's annoyance.

"She's got nothing to do with you," Randy said. "She's my... girlfriend."

"Right," Toby said. "Like you can afford a girlfriend like that."

"I ain't buying it either," Stonewall said. "She's way out of your league."

"She so far out of your league, she's in a completely different league," Toby sneered.

Stonewall turned to look at his nephew in disgust. Toby, taking the hint, nodded and took a step back.

"I swear to you," Randy said. "She's my new girlfriend. I met her online. She's in town visiting. Yeah, she's out of my league. And she's gonna probably figure that out soon enough, so I'm just enjoying it while I can."

He stopped to think.

"Wait. What do you even think I'm pulling over on you?"

Stonewall just shook his head, refusing to answer. Mainly because he had no answer. He was hoping Randy would call his bluff and confess.

"I think you may not be taking me serious enough," Stonewall growled.

He nodded to Toby, who grabbed Randy and locked his arms around his back. With Randy's arms restrained, Toby turned Randy toward Stonewall. Randy struggled but couldn't break Toby's lockhold. Stonewell grinned as he bunched his hand into a fist. But before he could throw a punch, he was interrupted by Jade, who had just walked out of the funeral home.

"Randy?" she said in her Texas accent, smiling innocently at Stonewall and Toby. "Are these your friends?"

42

Sheriff McKinley stepped out of his office, looking over the top of his reading glasses to survey the small sheriff station. A small desk was pushed up next to a see-through acrylic window to greet visitors. Two small sheriff deputy's desks were wedged in behind it with barely enough room to maneuver between the three. It was still early, so all three desks were currently unoccupied, although one of them shouldn't be. Sheriff McKinley walked toward the back of the office where a hallway led to holding cells but, more importantly, the coffeemaker.

"Jody?" he yelled out as he walked. "Where are you?"

He got his answer when he turned the corner. Sheriff's Deputy Jody Perry was standing at the counter, blowing on a freshly poured cup of coffee. Even though she was barely five feet tall, she had a stocky gymnast build that gave her an intimidating presence—a presence completely contradicted by the soft brown eyes that were presently peering over the top of her coffee cup.

"Did you run those prints yet?" Sheriff McKinley demanded.

He was clearly in a sour mood. Probably because he hadn't had much sleep. After his social visit had been cut short the night before, he had returned to the office where he had attempted to find and remove a fingerprint from the figurine goat he had nabbed from the store. It was normally a task that Jody or the other sheriff's deputy handled, but he didn't want to wait. However, after a couple of hours of searching for supplies and not sure how to scan and submit it, he decided to call it a night and turn the responsibility over to Jody in the morning.

His inability to complete such a simple task, coupled with his overly active suspicious imagination, had kept him awake the rest of the night. When Jody showed up to open the office at 5 a.m., she was surprised to see the sheriff already sitting at his desk.

"I'm working on it," Jody answered. "Just grabbing some coffee."

"Is there something there?" the sheriff asked.

Jody nodded.

"I got a pretty solid print and am fixing to send it over," she said. "Just wanted to get a little coffee first."

The sheriff grunted and she immediately sensed his impatience.

"I'll go do it right this second, sir."

"How long until you hear anything?" the sheriff asked.

Jody shrugged.

"Depends on their workload," she said. "But I'm getting it in early enough. We should hear back by noon."

The sheriff looked at the clock on the office wall. It was barely 8:00 a.m.

"You gonna tell me what this is for?" Jody asked. "The goat has me believing it has something to do with Clyde Philpot."

"What doesn't?" the sheriff deadpanned as he walked back into his office. "Let me know as soon as you hear something."

tonewall and Toby looked at the cute, disarming woman smiling back at them. Toby released his hold on Randy and Stonewall unclenched his fist. A big, shit-eating grin spread over his crinkled face.

"Well, looky who's here," he sneered.

Jade ignored him and walked casually over to Randy, kissing him on the cheek and wrapping her arm in his.

"Y'all come to pay respects to Clyde, too?" Jade asked innocently, laying on the accent—and the charm.

"We have a little unfinished business here with Randy," Stonewall said. "Your...boyfriend."

He wrapped the word 'boyfriend' in heavy quotations, making it clear he didn't believe the charade for a moment. But Jade kept up her naive facade.

"Oh, you can say anything in front of me," she said. "Randy and I don't have any secrets. Ain't that right, Honey?"

Randy, completely disoriented by the sudden shift in events, nodded blindly.

"This is private business, ma'am," Stonewall continued. "Man talk."

"Ohhhhhh. I'm sorry," Jade teased. "Because y'all are all men?"

She said it in such a non-threatening way it almost sounded like she was asking a sincere question. She released her arm from Randy's and stepped toward Stonewall, standing inches in front of him and looking him up and down. Then, in a lightning quick move, she grabbed Stonewall's crotch and squeezed hard. Stonewall yelped in agony, but Jade only tightened her grip.

"Whaddaya know?" she said with a smile. "You are a man. Just barely, though."

She gave her grip a hard twist before letting go. Stonewall gasped and fell to his knees, unable to even speak. Jade turned to a horrified Toby.

"You're not a man, are you?" she teased.

Toby shook his head nervously.

"No, ma'am," he stammered. "I mean, yes, ma'am. I mean... please don't hurt my balls!"

"Then get your friend and get the hell out of here," Jade hissed.

Toby nodded and frantically helped Stonewall to his feet, leading him back to their truck.

"You bitch," Stonewall yelled. "I'll cut that pretty little face to shreds. You're dead, Randy. You hear me? You're both dead!"

Randy stood, his mouth open in shock and fear as the rusty truck sputtered away. As soon as the truck left the parking lot, Jade patted Randy on the back and walked to the truck.

"Come on," she said. "Let's go."

Randy leaned forward, put his hands on his knees and began to hyperventilate.

"Oh, you've gone and done it now," he said.

"You're welcome," Jade replied sarcastically.

"Did you not just hear him?" Randy yelled. "He's going to kill me! I might as well just go inside and lay down in a coffin."

Jade turned to see the terrified look on Randy's face.

"Jesus, Randy. Calm down."

"You don't know who they are!" he yelled.

"I know exactly who they are," Jade snapped back. "They are the schoolyard bullies trying to take your lunch money. And they'll always take as much as you let them and won't stop until you stop them."

"But I can't stop them!" Randy yelled.

Jade let out a sigh and helped Randy to his truck, easing him into the driver's seat. She walked around to the other side and got in.

"Don't you ever get tired of being pushed around?" she asked.

"It ain't that simple," Randy argued.

"It's always that simple."

She handed the keys to Randy.

"No dice here," she said. "Your brother's clean."

She asked Randy if he knew of any other place beside the shop or the house where Clyde would have hid something. Any property. A boat. A cabin in the woods. The question distracted Randy and he was able to calm down. He told Jade the only property Clyde owned was The Lazy Goat and his truck.

How could I be so stupid? she thought.

Of course, she should check the man's truck. Other than the shop and his home, it was the next logical place. It definitely made more sense than a cavity search of his corpse. She was off her game. She was being *reactive* instead of *active*. It was time she took charge again.

"Where's his truck?" she asked.

44

A weathered old man sat on a crate of motor oil in front of the gas station, taking refuge in some morning shade and spitting black chewing tobacco at a curious squirrel. A black Ford F-150 pulled off the four-lane state highway and up to the single row of gas pumps in front of him.

Peter and Leo emerged from the large truck and the old man smirked at the sight of their business suits. He never understood suits. Especially in Texas. Why would you wear a jacket in the middle of summer? You wore jackets when you were cold. For that matter, why would you wear a noose around your neck? As far as the old man was concerned, it marked you as a fool.

"Well, it's pretty safe to say you boys ain't from around here," the old man said, punctuating it with another spit of tobacco. "Fill 'er up?"

"Where is Red Dirt?" Peter asked.

The Russian accent immediately caught the old man's attention. He slowly stood with a loud groan. His light blue coveralls were covered in oil and the name Ed was embroidered on the left chest.

"All you gotta do is look at the ground," Ed said. "There's red dirt everywhere."

He chuckled at his joke. Peter and Leo did not.

"We need to find town of Red Dirt," explained Leo. "Do you know of it...Ed?"

"I reckon I rightly do," Ed answered.

Leo and Peter waited for Ed to offer more.

"Then tell us," Peter said.

Ed laughed again, revealing a mouth of missing teeth.

"I'm just having some fun with you boys," he said. "Not too many people stop here. Not since that Buc-ee's went up down the road."

Realizing the two Russians were in no mood for chit-chat, Ed pointed down the highway.

"You just keep on the way you been going," he said. "Just stay on this service road and take a left on County Road 272. But it ain't marked. You just gotta look for the orange oil pump near the side of the road. Once you turn..."

He stopped and looked at Peter.

"You might wanna write this down," the old man grinned. "Come on inside. I'll write it down for ya. And you're gonna need gas."

"How far?" Peter asked.

The old man shrugged. "Depends on how fast you drive. Probably about six hours."

"Six hours!" exclaimed Peter. "That cannot be right!"

"Maybe it's three," Ed said. "I lost my watch."

He laughed again at his bad joke. Once again, Peter and Leo did not. Ed shook his head and walked inside.

"Don't they ever laugh where you're from?"

45

W illy's Last Bar sat just outside the city limits of Red Dirt, off of a small, single lane road barely wide enough for Randy's truck. Patches of grass on either side of the road were worn down from years of traffic moving out of the way for oncoming traffic. Randy had always been surprised there weren't more accidents on this stretch of asphalt that connected the bar to the main county road.

The building looked one termite short of being totally condemned. In fact, the only hints that it wasn't already an abandoned building were the neon beer signs in each of the four blackened windows. At night, they would cast a glow that could be seen from the main road.

Randy pulled his truck into the red clay dirt parking lot and chugged slowly past several parked cars that had been left the night before. Either by patrons that went home with someone else or that got too drunk to drive.

"You really think she'll be here?" Jade asked.

"She won't," Randy replied. "But Clyde's truck'll be."

Randy had told Jade that Amy Jo had arrived back in town

the day after Clyde's death and immediately claimed owner-
ship of the truck. Randy had no use for it, so he had just
handed her the keys. She had tried to lay claim to The Lazy
Goat as well, but it was technically owned by Mama. Plus, what
would she do with a shop that sold goats?

Randy drove around to the back of the bar, which was
clearly the establishment's dumping ground. Rather than try
and maneuver through the piles of trash, liquor bottles and
empty kegs, he parked the truck and suggested they walk. Jade
looked beyond the trash to an old white trailer home. Next to
the trailer were two trucks, a brown and white GMC and a
flashy red Ford with a giant decal of the Texas flag on the rear
window.

"There she is," Randy said, pointing to the red Ford.

As they neared Clyde's red truck, a throaty groan emerged
from the truck bed. Peering into the truck bed, they found Amy
Jo, sound asleep under a Texas A&M blanket she had hogged
for herself, leaving the pale, lanky man lying beside her fully
exposed. There were empty beer cans and scattered clothes all
around them, telling the tale that the sleeping couple weren't
likely to remember.

Randy shook his head in disgust. Jade put her finger to her
lips and motioned for Randy to go to the passenger side of the
truck while she opened the driver's door. They both quietly
looked through the truck's littered interior, sifting through
more beer cans, makeup, fast food bags, a box of condoms and,
finally, a purse.

Jade rifled through the purse, freezing when she heard the
couple stirring. Motioning for Randy to stay low, she quietly
and slowly peered up through the rear window and was
relieved to see the couple were still sleeping, but now Amy Jo's
hand lay flat over the man's face.

Jade and Randy returned to their search. The purse
contained nothing of interest. Neither did the glove compart-

ment. They were just about to give up hope, when Randy pulled a small paper bag from under the seat. He smiled and handed it to Jade.

"What the hell tarnation?" Amy Jo yelled from the back of the truck.

46

Amy Jo was on her knees in the bed of the truck, holding a blanket up over her body with one hand and using her other to point a small Smith & Wesson revolver through the rear window. The big Texas flag decal over the window disguised the identities of the truck's intruders so Amy Jo wasn't sure where to point the gun.

"Y'all get out of my truck right now," she yelled.

Randy immediately stepped away from the truck to reveal himself, his hands in the air.

"It's just me," he said.

Amy Jo looked at Randy confused as she tried to pull herself out of her still-drunk fog. The skinny man who had been sleeping beside her groaned as he woke up, clattering beer cans.

"What's going on?" he muttered as he looked for his pants.

"What the hell, Randy?" Amy Jo exclaimed, lowering her gun.

But when Jade stepped back from the driver's side of the car, the paper bag in hand, Amy Jo immediately raised the gun again. Jade resisted her immediate instinct to grab her own gun. Noticing Amy Jo's state, she knew she'd have no problem drawing first if she needed to. Luckily, Amy Jo recognized Jade from the restaurant and lowered her gun.

"I remember you," Amy Jo said.

"I just need to get something out of Clyde's truck," Randy exclaimed.

"It's my truck," Amy Jo corrected. "He give it to me."

Not wanting to argue, Randy nodded his head. "Fine. But I still need to get something."

"His brother left him something in the truck," Jade interrupted impatiently. "For the store. We didn't want to disturb you."

The man next to Amy Jo got up on all fours, unaware or uncaring of the fact that Amy Jo had been pointing a gun at two strangers.

"I can't find my boots," he muttered.

Amy Jo glanced at him and was immediately overcome with morning-after regret. She looked back at Randy, feeling his judgement.

"I'm just working out my grief," she said. "We all have our ways."

"No judgement here. In fact, I'm guessing you probably have some more grieving to do," Jade replied. "We found what we were looking for, so we'll be out of your...hair."

Amy Jo looked at the paper bag in Jade's hand and casually raised the pistol again—not necessarily to aim it at Jade, but just to make its presence known.

"See, the thing is...if it's in my truck, then it's technically mine."

Randy noticed Jade reaching a hand around to her own gun.

"It's nothing important," he said. "Just someone's order at the shop that I need to ship out."

Amy Jo's curiosity grew stronger.

"What is it?" she said, pointing at the bag with her gun.

Jade looked at Randy, her patience clearly running thin. Randy shook his head, pleading with her not to do anything rash. Jade let out a sigh and pulled out a handful of the small pendants.

"Oh, I love those little goats," Amy Jo squealed in delight. "They're so precious!"

Jade dropped them back in the bag and looked at Randy, making it clear that she wasn't going to put up with this any longer.

"I'd love to give them to you, but Clyde already sold 'em. But what about this?" Randy asked, trying one last appeal. "What if you get the money from the sale? That's fair, right?"

That seemed to get Amy Jo's attention.

"How much are we talking about?" she asked.

"Five hundred dollars," Jade said. "But they pay upon delivery, so we have to ship them out first."

"Five hundred?" Amy Jo exclaimed. "Are you shitting me?"

"But we gotta ship them out right away," Jade said, looking to Randy. "Right, Hon?"

Randy nodded. Amy Jo nodded, too, pretending to be smarter than she was.

"I imagine you have to pack them up with one of those certificates of authority," she said. "Like on QVC."

"Certificate of authenticity," Jade corrected, getting really annoyed with this woman.

Amy Jo rolled her eyes at Jade's grammar correction and dropped the gun.

"You better not be pulling a fast one over me, Randy Philpot," she said.

"You know me better than that," Randy said as he and Jade started walking back toward his truck.

"Excuse me, ma'am. Can you throw me that boot?" the man yelled out as Jade walked past a brown work boot.

She picked it up, turned and hurled it a little harder than necessary. As he ducked to avoid it, he accidentally yanked the blanket away from Amy Jo, exposing her naked body. She let out a yelp and immediately dropped out of sight.

47

The black pickup truck sat stubbornly on the side of the road with its hood up. Viktor leaned against the side of the truck, trying to remain calm. As the sun had risen higher in the sky, so had the temperature, and the crime boss had shed his suit coat and was even flirting with the thought of loosening his tie.

Leo and Peter, both tieless and with sleeves rolled up, were drenched in sweat.

"This is heat I've not known," Peter complained. "Why do people live in it?"

"Da. At least in cold you can put on coat," Leo replied as he looked at the engine in frustration.

"What do you think you will see in there?" Peter taunted his twin. "You know nothing about engines. It is clear we have run out of fuel."

"I told you we should have filled up at petrol station," Leo said.

"I did not trust it," Peter argued. "The petrol was probably watered down."

"This is not Russia," Leo argued back. "This is Texas. This is where they make petrol. Have you not seen oil towers everywhere."

"Would you both shut up?" Viktor snapped.

He looked down the empty, two-lane road in front of them, it's narrow path slicing through the countryside and disappearing into the woods.

"How much to go?" he asked.

Leo and Peter looked at each other, hoping the other had the answer. Peter finally spoke up.

"Eight kilometers?" he said.

Viktor nodded and took a deep inhale.

"Then we walk."

"It is getting hotter," Leo said.

Viktor ignored Leo and began to walk down the road with a cold determination. Leo and Peter scrambled to gather their guns and run after him.

s soon as Randy pulled his truck back on to the narrow road, Jade began to pull the small goat pendants from the bag, checking each one for a red dot.

"I thought he got rid of all of those," Randy said.

"He has more of these?" Jade asked as she continued her search.

"Gets 'em all the time," Randy explained. "Hands 'em out like candy. There'll probably be more than a few at the funeral," he said.

Jade pulled the last goat pendant out. No red dot.

"Damnit!" she yelled, throwing the entire bag on the floorboard in frustration.

Randy stared straight ahead, not sure what to do or say but afraid of making things worse. He could sense Jade's rage and worried she might take it out on him. Fortunately, she was distracted by the vibration of her cell phone. She looked at the incoming text and sighed, directing Randy to pull off to the side of the road. Without an explanation, she stepped out of the truck and made a call.

"Do you have it yet?" Donovan Fontaine asked upon answering the call.

"Not yet," Jade replied, trying to sound cool and in control. "But I've narrowed down the possibilities."

"I thought you said this would be in and out."

"Well, I've had to go further in than originally anticipated, but it's all under control."

"Viktor Petrov's flight landed in Dallas this morning," Donovan said.

Jade's heart sank. She had hoped she'd have more time.

"The good news is, he laid low in Dallas while a decoy unit sent the FBI off on a wild goose chase," Donovan continued. "That should buy you a little time."

"Do you have an ETA on when he'll get here?" Jade asked.

"Two hours? Three?"

Jade looked back at the truck, her mind speeding through a million possible solutions.

"They'll likely follow the same order of possible hiding places as I did, which will buy me a little more time," she said. "I've got one more move and then I'm bailing."

"Dare I ask what you have planned?" Donovan asked.

Jade rubbed the tension from the bridge of her nose.

"I'm going to a funeral."

49

D ean's rental car pulled into the empty parking lot of The Lazy Goat. He had now been up well over 24 hours and was running on fumes, adrenaline and lukewarm caffeine.

Staring at the store from inside his car, Dean's stomach did somersaults as he loaded a mag into the FBI-issued Glock 9mm he had never really used aside from target practice.

Finding the front door locked, he walked around to the back of the store and turned the knob of the rear entrance. He was surprised, but also relieved, to find that it opened easily.

He walked carefully through the back storeroom, his gun drawn and heart pounding. Other than target practice, which he still did regularly, he had never held a gun outside of training. He found himself mimicking cops on TV as he moved quietly, trying to hear more than his own heavy breathing.

He finally stopped at the entrance to the showroom. The sun gleamed through the showroom windows, bathing it in bright light. Even though he hadn't seen anyone inside when he had looked through the windows, he couldn't be certain. He also knew that, as soon as he stepped through the open doorway, he would be visible—and vulnerable—to anyone. So, he waited. Listening carefully for any sign of life.

Then he saw it.

A shadow moved quickly across the floor. Or at least that's what he thought he saw. If he was right, that would mean someone was standing just outside the door. Possibly Jade waiting for him to walk into a trap. He had two choices. He could retreat back in the showroom and try to draw her to him. He would not only be hidden in the dark, but he'd be able to see her when she stepped through the entry way. But he had a feeling Jade was too smart to do that. Which left him with his second option. He could use the element of surprise and confront her right now. Even if she were waiting to ambush him, she didn't know Dean was on to her. If he acted quickly, he could catch her off guard before she even knew what happened. It was definitely the more dangerous, reckless option. Maybe he did have a death wish. Or maybe he was tired of always retreating. Either way, he knew he'd rather go on the offense than fall back on the defense.

Before he could talk himself out of it, Dean gripped his gun with both hands, extended his arms and locked his elbows. He took a deep breath and spun through the entry way, pointing his gun toward his assailant.

"FBI. Freeze!" he yelled, realizing that the shadow person yelled "Freeze!" at the same time.

Standing three feet in front of him, with his own gun drawn, was a man in a sheriff's uniform.

"Drop your weapon," the sheriff yelled.

"I'm FBI," Dean yelled back, sweat pouring off his forehead.

The two men were both frozen, pointing their respective firearms at the other.

"Let's see some ID," the sheriff yelled.

Dean realized that the only risk he now faced was a

miscommunication with a trigger-happy local sheriff. He raised his gun in surrender.

"It's in my chest pocket," Dean said.

"Don't move," the sheriff yelled, still unsure. "Put your hands on the counter."

Dean nodded and turned toward the counter. He set the gun down gently and moved it away from his hands as a sign of surrender. The sheriff quickly pushed it even further away and, with his own pistol still trained on Dean, reached into the agent's chest pocket and pulled out his federal ID. When he realized that Dean was, in fact, a federal agent, Sheriff McKinley's shoulders dropped in a mixture of relief and disappointment.

He gave Dean his ID back and slid his gun back to him.

"You could have gotten yourself killed," the sheriff admonished.

"I could say the same," Dean said back.

"Can I ask what you're doing snooping around a closed store?" the sheriff asked.

"I have reason to believe that a very dangerous woman may be in your town," Dean replied.

The sheriff grinned, his suspicions validated.

"I think we have a lot to talk about."

50

Having left in such a rush earlier, Randy was fully prepared to face the wrath of his mother. But when he and Jade walked into the house, the only thing that hit him was the unmistakable smell of cabbage and onions.

"Randall?" Mama's voice yelled from the kitchen. "That'd better be you."

Randy and Jade walked into the kitchen to find Mama, still wearing her blue housedress and giant rollers, standing over the stove and stirring a large pot.

"You better have a damn good reason for leaving me like a turd on a toadstool this morning."

Randy started to give his mom the excuse he had practiced the entire drive back from Willy's, but Jade interjected.

"We're sorry, Mama," she said with a thick helping of Southern sincerity. "Randy was just so upset about his brother that I told him he needed to go grieve for a little while. So he could be strong enough for you later. It was my fault."

Mama looked up at Jade's forlorn face. Randy stood behind her and nodded solemnly, hoping it would be enough to pacify his mother. When he saw her stern expression start to melt, he knew it worked.

"Oh my Lord, come here child," she said to Randy, holding up her arms to take him in for a bear hug. "In all my grieving and dealing with everything, I totally forgot how this was hurting you, too."

"You got enough on your plate, Mama," Randy added. "I didn't want to add my burden to yours."

Mama kissed her son tenderly on the forehead.

"Clyde touched us all," Mama said. "I appreciate you doing it on your own time. But in the future, you need to let me in on your plans. You hear?"

Randy nodded.

"Speaking of plates," she said as she released Randy and turned her attention back to the pot in front of her. "You're just in time for lunch."

"Don't we have to get ready for the funeral?" Randy asked.

"You need food," Mama said.

She yelled out for Pauline, who shuffled in wearing an old terrycloth robe, bright red lipstick and her perpetually askew wig. She smiled at Randy and Jade and plopped down in one of the four chairs that were positioned around a small red table. Mama ladled out the contents of the pot in a bowl, then sat it down in front of Pauline.

"Here you go, Pauline," Mama said.

"I hate boiled cabbage" Pauline griped.

"You loved it yesterday. Look. I even put the little marshmallows in it to sweeten it up for you," Mama replied matter of factly. "You two sit down."

"We've got a lot to do," Randy protested. "Jen needs something to wear to the funeral."

Mama stopped mid-ladle and looked at Jade.

"Who comes to a funeral and don't bring no clothes?" she asked.

Before Jade could reply, Mama pointed to the table, shaking her head.

"You can borrow something from Pauline," she said. "But you're gonna eat first."

Unsure what to do, Randy looked at Jade for permission. He was serving two masters now and it was beginning to overwhelm him. Jade nodded and Randy let out a sigh of relief. The couple sat down, disgustingly mesmerized by Pauline, who would slurp up a piece of cabbage then spit half of it back in the bowl. After a few half-hearted half-slurps, she pushed the bowl away.

"I'm full," she scowled.

Mama snatched the bowl away and Jade watched as she poured the half-eaten cabbage back in the pot. Then, without missing a beat, she ladled out another helping from the same pot and sat it in front of Jade. Jade looked down at the recycled cabbage stew. Half-melted mini-marshmallows floated in the concoction and Jade could actually see Pauline's lipstick stains on some of the cabbage.

"We only got leftovers until Randy can get the shop back in order," Mama explained.

"I'm selling the shop, Mama," Randy said. "It loses more money than it makes."

"You will do no such thing," Mama snapped as she sat a bowl in front of her son. "That's your brother's legacy and you're gonna honor it."

Jade watched as Randy spooned up his own lipstick-painted cabbage and marshmallow stew and ate it without hesitation. Mama sat down on the other side of her and began slurping up her serving. Jade had traveled all over the world and had eaten all kinds of bizarre and exotic foods without flinching. Live bugs in the Amazon rainforest. Tuna eyeballs in Japan. Monkey brains in India. Maybe it was the odd combination of questionable ingredients. Maybe it was knowing her lunch had been spit up by a geriatric toothless woman. Or maybe it was the sound of Randy and Mama's slurp symphony being performed in stereo on either side of her. For some reason, this meal was going to require all the discipline and concentration Jade could muster. She lifted a spoonful to her lips, looking up just as Pauline removed her teeth to dislodge a piece of cabbage from them.

Once Jade forced herself past the mental barrier of knowing she was eating someone else's spit-up, she was surprised to find the soup wasn't half bad. She would slit anyone's throat that tried to force her to eat it again, but she had eaten worse foods in her life.

After demanding that everyone stop and eat lunch, Mama was now panicked that they were running late.

"Everyone is gonna be looking at us," she had warned. "Do not embarrass me."

She took Jade by the hand and led her into Pauline's room, where she rifled through the closet until she found what she was looking for. Pulling something off a hanger, she held it out in front of Jade. It was a floor-length, black evening dress that was probably very fashionable...in the early seventies. If the super-sized lapels and ornate gold button trim didn't immediately date it, then the stiff double-knit polyester material did.

"This used to be one of Pauline's," Mama said.

Jade looked over Mama's shoulder, hoping to find an alternative hanging in the closet.

"But my sister used to be a real head-turner," Mama said, sifting through the memories that the dress awoke.

She handed the dress to Jade and grabbed a framed photo off of a shelf. It was an old black and white photo of a beautiful woman and a handsome man. They both looked like movie stars.

"That was her husband," Mama said, handing the photo to Jade. "Right after they got married. He got killed in Vietnam."

She took the photo back and placed it gently on the shelf.

"She never remarried but I guarantee you she was still turning heads up until not that long ago," Mama continued. "Nobody can outrun age, I guess. Anyway, this dress'll look good on you. A black dress never goes out of style. And you can barely see the stains."

Jade held the dress out in front of her and Mama turned back to the closet, pulling down a shoe box from a shelf.

"She got shoes to match," Mama said. "I'm hoping they fit. If not, you can go barefoot. Lots of folks do in the summer."

She handed the shoe box to Jade.

"You're gonna look beautiful no matter what," she said gently.

Jade actually felt her cheeks blush.

"Randall really likes you," Mama said. "I can tell."

Jade wasn't sure how to respond.

"You don't gotta say nothing," Mama said. "I see the way he looks at you. And I see the way you look back. It ain't the same. But that's okay. It'll come with time. He's a good man."

"He is," Jade found herself saying.

And she meant it. Randy had been a pain in the ass, but it was clear he was a good person. Decent and caring. He could use a little bit of backbone, but with someone like Mama whipping him down, Jade could see why he had such little confidence.

"He sure does love you," Jade said. "Maybe a little too much."

What am I doing? she thought. *Do not get this lady riled up. Do not get involved.*

"There ain't no such thing as a boy loving his mama too much," Mama replied with a smile.

"Well, except if it stops him from being all the man he should be," Jade said, speaking slowly and carefully. "There are things he wants to do with his life, but he's afraid you'll hate him for going after them."

Even though she tried to hide it, Mama was clearly shocked by what she was hearing.

"That's just foolish talk," she said. "I would never stand in his way. Hell, I worked two jobs just so he could go off to school to be an eye doctor and then he just up and quits."

"He came back to help take care of you," Jade pointed out. "After your husband died."

Mama was visibly shaken, but was growing more defensive.

"You don't know," she said. "Who are you coming in my house and telling me about my son?"

Jade nodded.

"You're right. I'm way out of line and I apologize."

Mama immediately softened. She laid the dress out on the bed to give her something to do.

"So what is it he wants to do?"

Jade told Mama about the deep-sea charter in Florida and how it was a once-in-a-lifetime opportunity to get in on. She even suggested that it could be very lucrative and could set Mama and Pauline up really nice. Mama listened, remaining expressionless throughout the entire pitch. When Jade was finished, she just nodded and turned for the door.

"We need to leave in twenty minutes," she said, not even acknowledging what Jade had told her. "So, no lollygagging."

52

S heriff McKinley sat at the counter of Perty's while Agent Bennet paced outside on his phone. The sheriff had filled the FBI agent in on the suspicious new girlfriend that had shown up in town. There were no matches to the fingerprint he had lifted from the figurine, but all that meant was that Jen wasn't in the system. Or Jade, as the agent had called her. He had shown the sheriff the fuzzy picture from the Russian hotel but there was nothing about it that matched the blonde woman supposedly from Dallas. Still, the thought of an international jewel thief in his county excited the sheriff. Other than an occasional drunk and disorderly or domestic squabble, there wasn't that much crime in Red Dirt. He was having a hard time believing Clyde was some sort of international smuggler. With ties to the Russian mob, no less.

Dean was yelling so loudly into his phone that the sheriff could hear him inside.

"How did they lose them?"

He had called Agent Chin, who had been keeping tabs on Viktor Petrov and the twins, only to find out that they had given local agents the slip.

"What do you mean low priority?" he went on. "Yes, I'm sure they're heading here. Jade's been here, Kevin. And if she's here, then it's where Viktor Petrov is heading... No, I haven't seen her. But the local sheriff has... No, I can't prove it's her but who else could it be?...How long?...Just, please. Do your best."

Dean hung up his phone and walked back inside, where the bemused sheriff was waiting.

"That didn't seem to go well," the sheriff said.

"So where is Jade now?" Dean asked.

"She stayed the night at Lucille Philpot's place," the sheriff said. "I escorted her there myself."

"Oh my God," Dean said. "That poor family."

The sheriff raised his hand to calm him.

"Everyone's fine. I checked on 'em this morning and she was already gone. Took off with Lucille's son, Randy."

A waitress appeared in front of the men with two slices of pie.

"Oh, I didn't order anything," Dean said.

"Trust me," the sheriff replied, nodding to the waitress to set them down.

"Are you saying she's taken a hostage?" Dean asked.

The sheriff chuckled. "Mama, that's what everybody calls Lucille, said she caught 'em sleeping out in the yard this morning. Cozy as can be. Next thing she knew, they drove off somewhere."

"You know where they went?" Dean asked.

"No, but don't worry. Randy ain't gonna run out on his mama. Not today, for sure."

"You don't know Jade," Dean replied.

"You don't know Mama," the sheriff smiled. "I suggest we just hang tight here. I got a pretty good idea where they're gonna wind up."

He motioned out the window toward the First Baptist

Church. Cars were already starting to pull into the parking lot for Clyde Philpot's funeral service.

Dean looked at the church as he took a bite of pie.

"Oh my God," he exclaimed, spinning around to face the sheriff. "This pie is delicious!"

The sheriff nodded and watched the FBI agent devour the rest of the pie. Over the course of the next half hour, the two men sat and waited. From their vantage point, they could see everyone that entered the church. Dean ordered a second slice of pie and the sheriff introduced him to some of the other patrons in the restaurant. The FBI agent was immediately taken in by their Southern hospitality. He started asking questions about their lives. The community. The more he learned, the more he became enamored with Red Dirt. He became so wrapped up in his conversations that he almost missed the arrival of Randy's truck.

The sheriff nudged him and pointed to it. Dean watched as the foursome exited the truck. When the blonde woman in the odd black dress slid out of the passenger seat, he caught his breath. She didn't look anything like any of the other pictures. But he knew. He had finally found Jade.

53

The church was packed, every wooden pew filled with the residents of Red Dirt and neighboring communities. As the owner and sole employee of The Lazy Goat, Clyde Philpot was well-known in the area. Plus, a funeral was as big of a social event as you'd get in Red Dirt. Most everyone jumped at the chance to dress up and pay their respects. Everyone else showed up because they were afraid of what Mama would do to them if they didn't.

Mama's friends from Perty's restaurant were there, trading gossip and passing judgement on everyone that entered the church. Amy Jo had cleaned up as well as she could, but makeup could only cover up a hangover so much. She sat beside her friend Suzy, who seemed to have "grieved" just as hard the night before. Pooter and Eunice Carter from the hardware store were there. They had closed shop for the afternoon in honor of Clyde. It wasn't that huge of a gesture, considering all of their customers were also at the funeral. Even Stonewall and Toby sat respectfully in one of the back pews.

The early afternoon sun shone through one of the two stained glass windows, creating a rainbow mosaic of colors on the large cross that hung on the wall behind the alter. Two large fake ferns sat in tall stands on either side of the cross, one of them half concealing the church organ. In front of all of it was the preacher's podium and in front of the podium was Clyde's casket. It was half open, and Clyde was sleeping peacefully in a light blue suit, his hair uncharacterically combed and styled. It was probably the most presentable he'd ever looked. Fortunately, the bottom half of the casket remained closed, so Mama would never know he still wasn't wearing any shoes.

Everyone waited in respectful anticipation and the only sounds were quiet murmurs punctuated by an occasional cough. Mama had requested that the family be seated last, brought in like at a wedding procession. It was something she had seen at her Cousin Judith's funeral and she liked everything about it. It not only gave her the sympathetic attention she felt she deserved, but it also was the perfect vantage point for her to see who all had shown up. Or, more importantly, who hadn't.

There had been a small pre-funeral argument between Amy Jo and Mama. Amy Jo felt she should be part of the immediate family promenade, having been Clyde's wife. But Mama wasn't having it. She told Amy Jo that she had lost that privilege when she divorced her son. Amy Jo countered with the argument that it was Clyde who filed for divorce, to which Mama reminded the hungover blonde that he did that because she had up and run off with the bass player of a visiting country band.

"He weren't even the singer!" Mama had yelled.

Amy Jo had finally backed down after negotiating the chance to deliver a short eulogy during the service. Mama had given her four minutes.

With that settled and everyone seated, the family waited in the back of the church for their cue. As self-concious as Jade was in her outfit, she was easily—and purposefully—upstaged by Mama, who was wearing a long black dress with billowy chiffon lace sleeves and whose silver hair had been styled into a wavy bouffant that somehow defied all laws of gravity. Pauline was dressed surprisingly out of character in a simple black pant suit. Other than her still-askew auburn wig and bright red lipstick, she almost looked normal. Jade also couldn't help but take notice of Randy. Showered, shaved and dressed in a black suit, she realized for the first time how handsome he really was.

It had been decided that Jade and Pauline would walk in together, followed by Randy and his mother. As the organist played the first familiar notes of Amazing Grace, the two women linked arms and began the procession. Pauline, happy to get out of the house, waved at people she knew as if she were in a parade. Jade scoured the crowd, looking for goat pendants. Spotting one on a necklace of an elderly woman sitting by the aisle, Jade faked a stumble and grabbed the woman to catch her balance, ripping off the pendant in the process. She quickly realized it had no red dot and handed it back to the woman, apologizing for her clumsiness. Pauline began to cackle hysterically, and Jade continued the walk to the front of the church. It was a stupid move and she immediately regretted it. She had gambled on the first goat she saw and had accomplished nothing more than drawing extra attention to herself.

Luckily, Mama made sure everyone's attention quicky shifted to her. She entered on Randy's arm, sobbing just loud enough for everyone to hear, nodding sad hellos at her friends and making mental notes of who all was there and what they were wearing.

Not that her sadness was an act. If anything, the funeral had brought the reality of the situation down on her. She was burying her oldest son. He wasn't a golden child by any stretch of the imagination, but he was her firstborn. She was always entertained by his wild dreams and ambitions and loved being able to be there for him when he regularly fell short of them.

He was a charmer that doted on his mother and always found a way to make her laugh. He had also been the son that stuck around. Randy had gone off to college for a while, but Clyde had stayed right by his mother's side through thick and thin. In fact, Mama couldn't remember him ever being away more than a couple of days. And now he was gone forever.

Randy slid in the pew and helped his mother sit down before sitting down next to Jade. They listened quietly, looking at Clyde laying in rest before them as the organist finished the gospel hymn. People rustled and stirred in their seats, preparing for the service. No one really noticed the FBI agent and local sheriff slip in and take a spot standing against the back wall.

Once silence fell on the room, Pastor McCoy, an old frail man who easily in his late 80s, shuffled solemnly — and slowly — to the podium.

54

Pastor McCoy leaned on the pulpit and looked across the congregation with what Jade first thought was a scornful gaze, as if he was personally damning every person in his church to hell. She soon realized that was just his normal expression.

A preacher with resting judgement face, Jade thought to herself with a slight smile.

As if he sensed her amusement, the pastor turned to look directly at her, and Jade looked down in shame. There's something about a preacher behind a pulpit that can trigger guilt in even the most guiltless.

Pastor McCoy lowered his head and shut his eyes in what Jade assumed was the beginning of a silent prayer. With everyone's head bowed, she would be able to look around the crowd for more goat pendants. But everyone seemed to watch the pastor patiently.

He's not praying, Jade realized. *He's gathering his thoughts. Or taking a short nap.*

Finally, he raised his head slowly and began to speak. For

having such a feeble, old body, his voice was surprisingly deep and authoritative.

"I ain't gonna put lipstick on a pig," the pastor said. "Clyde Philpot was a man with many faults and a lifelong struggle with temptation. But the Good Lord knows that, underneath it all, he was a God-fearing man. And I can say with righteous confidence that, right now, Clyde Philpot is sitting up in heaven playing a game of Texas Hold'em with the angels. I just pray he don't cheat."

A murmur of laughter spread through the congregation. The preacher continued, his eulogy singularly seeming to focus on reassuring everyone that Clyde hadn't gone to hell. Finally, he asked everyone to stand and bow their heads. As he began to pray, Jade seized the opportunity to look around. It was hard to see everyone from her vantage point, but she could make out what seemed to be goat pendants hanging around the necks of several women. She made a mental note of each of them. Where they were sitting. Who was sitting with them. When the funeral was over, she would have to act fast to check them all before they left.

Jade craned her neck to see a little better and locked eyes with a ten-year-old boy who had also chosen to ignore the pastor's directions. They stared at each other and the kid smirked, as if to acknowledge their joint membership in a secret club. Then Jade noticed someone else looking directly at her. From his white, short-sleeved dress shirt and black slacks, she immediately tagged him as a fed. She turned back around, trying to process this kink in her plan. Maybe it was a coincidence. Maybe he just lived here. Or maybe he knew Clyde from his many brushes with the law. But she knew what was most likely. What made the most sense. The FBI was investigating Clyde's involvement with stolen jewelry trafficking. Regardless, it was a complication that Jade would have to account for.

Then something else caught her attention. Mama was

holding something white. She clutched it tight so it was hard to be sure, but Jade felt pretty confident it was a goat. She barely noticed as the pastor signaled the end of his prayer with a solemn "amen" which was then echoed by a very unenthusiastic amen from the congregation.

Jade elbowed Randy and nodded toward the object in Mama's hand. A look of panic shot over his face as he realized what she was holding.

The pastor had paused again. Jade wasn't sure if it was for effect or if he was actually saving up energy to speak, which he finally did.

"Clyde's wife," he finally said.

"EX-wife!" Mama corrected loudly.

"Clyde's ex-wife, Amy Jo Billings, would now like to share a few precious memories with us."

Mama shook her head in silent protest. Even though she had agreed to it, she had no intention of showing her approval of Amy Jo's involvement. Randy patted her hand to calm her, and also get a better look at the porcelain object in her hand. She nervously played with it, giving Jade the opportunity to get a better look. There was no red dot.

Disappointed yet again, she turned her attention to Amy Jo, who was walking slowly from her seat to the front of the church. She paused at the single step leading up to the podium as if it were a mountain and a tall man sitting near her stood and assisted her to the podium. Jade could tell Amy Jo was acting half out of overdramatic grief, partly because she was still visibly drunk, but mainly because she could barely walk in her skintight, extremely short red dress and matching stiletto heels.

She was also wearing a goat pendant.

55

E veryone in Red Dirt was at Clyde's funeral. So, when three well-dressed but very sweaty men trudged into town by foot, there was no one around to notice them.

Viktor Petrov walked tall and proud, showing no sign he had just walked five miles in the Texas heat, other than a dress shirt completely drenched in sweat. He was even still wearing his tie, although he had finally loosened it a bit.

Peter and Leo were not hiding their discomfort nearly as well. Both men had tossed their ties miles ago. Peter had attempted to maintain a strand of decorum to match his boss's, but he was three times as sweaty, and his shirt was unbuttoned down to his navel. Leo didn't even try to care. He had untucked his shirt somewhere along the way and even unbuttoned it, revealing a particularly hairy chest. A newly formed blister had formed on his foot causing him to limp and wince with every step.

The three Russians took curious note of the silence as they walked through The Lazy Goat parking lot. Looking around, Viktor pointed to the packed church parking lot located on the far side of the intersection from them.

"The Texans," he said. "They love their church. They call this part of America the Bible Belt."

"This must be the buckle," Peter mumbled, trying to catch his breath.

The men looked inside the store windows and, when they felt confident the building was empty, Leo kicked the door in. The three men were hit by a blast of cool, air-conditioned air and they stood in the doorway, bathing in the sweet relief. Shutting the door, and the sweltering heat, behind them, they took in the disaster of the ransacked showroom.

"Why would one store have so much goat?" Peter asked.

"We are too late," Viktor grumbled. "She has already been here."

56

A my Jo walked behind the pulpit, dramatically composing herself. Her face pinched as she tried to force tears, but when that effort proved fruitless, she just pretended to cry, wiping imaginary tears from her dry cheeks.

"I never stopped loving you, Clyde Philpot," she said, looking down at the casket. "Not even when I had gone off to spread my creative wings."

"More like, 'spread her legs'," Mama whispered loudly out of the side of her mouth.

"You were always there for me," Amy Jo continued. "And I always knew you were by my side, no matter where I went."

"Or whose back seat you were rolling around in," Mama commented again.

Randy elbowed his mother gently to get her to quiet down and his mother slapped at his arm. But Jade barely noticed. She was staring at Amy Jo's pendant. As if Amy Jo could sense it, she began to play with the small goat dangling around her neck.

"He gave me this pendant right before he died," Amy Jo said. "Because I was his one and only."

Amy Jo didn't even notice all the other women in the congregation who instinctively reached up to touch their own identical pendants.

"I will always wear it close to my heart," Amy Jo said.

And, as she lifted the pendant to her lips, Jade noticed a small red dot on the back. She sat up, fighting the instinct to immediately storm the stage and grab it. She needed to be patient. There were too many people around, including an FBI agent. She would corner Amy Jo after the service and take it then. As people all mingled and shared condolences she would be able to slip away without anyone noticing. Her heart began to beat faster, knowing her hunt was coming to an end.

"Like Preacher McCoy said, he was a good man," Amy Jo went on. "He was a gentle, loving man. In all our time together, I only had to call the law on him once."

She looked down at Clyde's restful, not very life-like face in the casket.

"I worked at Ginger Snaps when I met him," she said. "As soon as I looked into his eyes, I knew he was the one. I didn't dance for nobody else the rest of the night."

She motioned to her friend Suzy, who had been standing to the side of the alter. Suzy helped Amy Jo down the step so that she was standing at the foot of the casket. She then walked back up to the pulpit, positioning a smartphone next to the microphone.

Amy Jo spoke directly to Clyde. "This was the song that was playing when we first locked eyes. I love you always, Clyde."

It would have been a very private moment, other than the fact that Amy Jo spoke loud enough for everyone to hear her. She then nodded at Suzy and her friend pressed a button on the phone. A heavy metal power ballad began to blast through the speakers and Amy Jo shut her eyes and began to gently sway to the music.

As electric guitar chords were punctuated by pounding

drums, Amy Jo began to lose herself in the music. Her hips began to sway a little more suggestively. Her hands moved sensuously over her body as the sway evolved into a grind. As the song took her back, she began to dance as if she was still in Ginger Snaps and it wasn't long before she was stripping with her clothes on.

The men and younger boys took notice, shifting in their seats. The man who had assisted Amy Jo up to the podium seemed to fall in a trance and instinctively reached for his wallet. His wife slapped his hand as he started to pull out a dollar bill.

Finally, it became too much for Mama. She bolted up and stormed the podium, throwing the smartphone across the room. The music stopped abruptly, yanking Amy Jo out of her trance. She looked up at Mama who was now marching back down off the podium and toward her.

"How dare you turn my son's funeral into a tramp dance!" she yelled. "You never deserved Clyde and you sure as hell don't deserve that necklace."

She grabbed for it, but Amy Jo took a step back, clutching it. Jade stood up. This was getting out of hand. She looked back at the FBI agent standing next to the sheriff. His eyes were trained on her, and she immediately realized he knew who she was.

She had no choice. She had to make her move. Now.

57

Amy Jo tripped backward, accidentally planting her hand on Clyde's face to catch her fall. Mama screamed in horror and her face twisted into a rage and fury so intense, people in the first two pews started clammering to get out of the way.

Randy leapt to his feet and tried to pull his mother back, but she swatted him away like a mosquito, her eyes locked on Amy Jo. Unable to get past Randy and Mama, Jade ran up and around the podium and down the other side. As Pauline laughed in delight at the chaos, Jade lunged at Amy Jo from behind. They both tumbled forward, knocking the casket off its stand. It toppled to the ground with them, and Clyde's body half-rolled out on to the floor.

The entire congregation stood in shock, standing to get a better view of the commotion and unwittingly blocking Dean and the sheriff, who were now trying to struggle through the crowd. Some parishioners had pulled Jade off of Amy Jo and were holding her back. Others were restraining Mama. Amy Jo clutched her goat pendant.

"What is wrong with you people?" she yelled.

Stonewall and Toby stood up. Stonewall was tall enough that he could see Amy Jo's pendant was the source of the pandemonium. He had no idea why, but he figured it must be because it held some value. And he wanted in on it.

"Get that!" he yelled to Toby, pointing to the pendant.

The two men began to maneuver around the outside aisle of the church in order to get around the gathering crowd.

"Give me that pendant," Jade growled.

Horrified and confused, Amy Jo let out a panicked scream and ran through a side door behind the podium that led to a fellowship hall. Jade wrestled free and chased after her, as did Randy, Mama, Stonewall and Toby. Pauline pushed through the crowd.

"Wait for me," Pauline yelled, still laughing.

She was followed closely by Dean and the sheriff.

The rest of the congregation stood in shock, staring down at Clyde's body, not quite sure what had just happened. They were distracted by the muffled voice of Pastor McCoy.

"Help me!" he pleaded.

It was coming from underneath the toppled casket. Several men scrambled to move the casket and free the old man. As they moved the casket, Clyde's body rolled out of his forever home. The crowd let out a collective gasp and an elderly woman at the front of the crowd passed out.

As the men helped Pastor McCoy to his feet, the ten-year-old boy pointed at Clyde's corpse.

"He ain't got no shoes on!"

58

A my Jo had kicked off her stiletto heels in the fellowship hall before scrambling out the back door. She was already terrified of Mama but now Randy's new girlfriend was some kind of maniac, too. Driven by adrenaline and fear, she ran in a panic, high-tailing it toward the first place she saw: The Lazy Goat.

She was being chased by a small mob of people who were all shouting things at her but she couldn't hear them over her own hysterical screams. It was just as well. Had she been able to hear them, she would have been even more confused.

"Amy Jo, please!" Randy begged.

"Get her!" Stonewall demanded.

"Stop, FBI!" Dean announced.

"You tramp!" Mama yelled.

Jade wasn't yelling. She was focused on catching the crazed woman who was attempting to run in a tight red skirt. Jade's outfit was creating its own obstacles. The floor-length dress and high heels made it hard for her to run at full speed. Never breaking stride, she kicked off the shoes and held the hem of the dress above her knees as she took off after the hysterical ex-wife.

Amy Jo reached The Lazy Goat and yanked the door open, running inside but then stopping dead cold in her tracks. A very sweaty man in nice clothes was pointing a gun directly at her chest. She froze in shock and raised her hands.

Jade was the next to race into the store. As soon as she entered, she saw Peter pointing a gun at Amy Jo and knew what was going on. She wasn't surprised when she felt Viktor's gun pointing at her temple. She sighed and raised her hands.

Dean was next, but he had caught a glimpse of someone pointing a gun at Jade and had rushed in prepared. With his own gun drawn, he burst in the door yelling "FBI" and aimed his gun at Viktor, only to feel Leo's gun pressed against his own temple.

They were almost barreled down by Randy, who ran in next. Seeing all the guns drawn, he immediately raised his hands in surrender.

"Don't shoot!" he pleaded.

Stonewall and Toby were the next to race inside. They immediately pulled out their own revolvers, pointing them back and forth between the three Russians.

Sheriff McKinley was right behind them, his gun drawn and pointed at Jade.

"Gotcha," he yelled, before realizing he was late to the pistol party.

Leo pulled out a second pistol and aimed it at the sheriff. The group stood frozen, everyone silently assessing the precarious situation. Viktor was the first to speak. He moved in front of Jade and smirked.

"Jade, my lovely," he purred. "It is so good to see you. Although, I am a bit surprised. I thought you preferred to work alone."

Dean heard the name Jade and muttered "I knew it" under his breath.

"And now you see why," Jade replied coldly.

Viktor smiled and looked Jade up and down.

"Nice dress," he said sarcastically.

He motioned toward Amy Jo, her hands still in the air.

"I see you found my package," he said. "I am most grateful for the personal delivery."

He walked to Amy Jo, gun still trained on Jade, and examined her pendant, noticing the red dot.

"I'll take that," he said.

His hand slithered lightly down her neck and the front of her chest to the pendant. But before he could get a solid grip on it, Amy Jo fell to the floor in a dead faint. The goat pendant was yanked out of Viktor's hand and it crashed to the floor, shattering on impact and releasing a beautiful blue diamond the size of a fifty-cent coin. Everyone except Viktor and Jade gasped in awe at the sparkling treasure. But the pause was quickly interrupted when a furious Mama stormed through the door.

59

"Where is she?" Mama demanded, oblivious to all the guns pointed at everyone.

The distraction was just what Jade needed. In a blink of the eye, she did a front flip, kicking Viktor's gun from his hand. As she landed, she punched the Russian mob boss in the nose, knocking him to the floor. As she hoped, the attack created a chain reaction and total chaos ensued.

Peter fired at Dean just as he dove to the floor. The shot missed, shattering one of the windows at the front of the store. Dean rolled across the floor as the sheriff traded shots with Leo, but as everyone had begun to run for cover, they both missed their targets as well. In a fit of panic, Stonewall and Toby opened fire on Peter and Leo, hitting nothing but a wall of goat figures that the Russians had ducked behind.

In the middle of the mayhem, Mama stood in shock, guns blazing all around her, until Randy yanked her to the floor. As she fell, the sheriff noticed Pauline had been standing behind her and he pulled her to the ground, scrambling to get her out of harm's way.

Everyone took cover as they continued to exchange gunfire,

shattering goat figurines and exploding light fixtures. It was all over in a matter of seconds. Everyone had taken cover behind counters and shelves and the explosive pops of gunfire were replaced by the flaccid clicks of empty gun chambers.

Randy had pulled Mama behind the sales counter where Dean had also taken cover.

"Can someone tell me what the Sam Hill is going on here?" Mama demanded. "Who are you people and why are you shooting up my son's store?"

"Ma'am, I need you to calm down," Dean whispered loudly. "I'm FBI. And these men are very dangerous."

Viktor's voice called out from the far side of the store.

"Give me Jade and the diamond and no one has to die," he demanded.

"Who the hell is Jade?" Mama asked.

"Where the hell is Jade?" Dean muttered.

Dean peeked around the edge of the sales counter. Other heads poked up from behind shelves like a coterie of prairie dogs.

"Boss, look," Leo muttered loudly enough for everyone to hear.

Dean looked at Amy Jo's passed out body in the middle of the showroom and knew immediately what the Russian was referring to.

The diamond was gone.

60

An old, pale-blue Dodge pickup bounced and clanked down one of the narrow asphalt backroads that led out of Red Dirt. The driver, an old farmer in a plaid work shirt and a tattered gray baseball hat, whistled to himself as he drove. Sitting next to him was a large brown and black hound with a droopy face and giant ears. The dog leaned her head out of the open window and the breeze caught her constant drool and sprayed it back.

Jade sat on the other side of the truck bed to avoid the shower of hound spit. Her black dress was torn up a bit, but she appeared unscathed otherwise. She looked down at her clinched fist and finally relaxed her grip to look at the large blue diamond.

She had to admit that, for a minute, she thought she had reached the end of the line. She had been expecting Viktor Petrov to show up at some point, but not the FBI. As luck had it, having them both there at the same time is what gave her the opportunity to grab the diamond and make her escape. They would keep each other busy for a while, which would buy her enough time to get far away. It was actually as clean a getaway as she could expect.

She looked down at her evening dress and noticed a small rip just above the knee. She dug a finger in the hole and pulled at the fabric until it ripped. She would be able to get new clothes soon enough but, for now, she needed to make her outfit a bit more comfortable. She was pretty sure Pauline would understand.

She reached under her dress to the back of the waistband of the biker shorts she was wearing. While she had left her gun in Randy's truck, she was able to store her phone under her dress. Unfortunately, there was no cell reception. She would have to text Donovan later.

She sat back and smiled, letting out a loud sigh as she watched the road grow longer behind her. Still, she couldn't shake the very unfamiliar feeling of guilt that was beginning to claw at her.

61

Viktor, Peter and Leo remained hidden behind a tall shelf of shattered ceramics as they reloaded. On the other side of the store, behind the checkout counter, Dean reloaded his Glock. He crawled past Randy and Mama and peered around the side of the counter to look for the sheriff. Behind a toppled display, near the shot-out window, he could make out the tan shirt of McKinley's uniform. The shoulder appeared stained in crimson. He must have been shot.

"Are you okay?" Dean called out in a loud whisper.

The sheriff had been trying to collect himself after the gun battle when he heard Dean's question. He signaled to the FBI agent that he was okay. Luckily, the bullet had just grazed his shoulder. It hurt like hell but nothing the proud sheriff couldn't bear. Truth be told, he was wearing his first battle scar proudly.

He looked at a wide-eyed Pauline who was sitting next to him and put a finger to his lips to instruct her to remain quiet. Then he whispered into his shoulder radio.

"Jody, this is the Sheriff. We got ourselves a bit of a situation."

He instructed the sheriff's deputy to keep the funeral crowd away from The Lazy Goat and block off the area. He also needed her to reach out to the Campbell County Sheriff's Department for backup immediately.

"We're gonna need an ambulance, too," he finished, looking at Amy Jo's passed out body.

He asked Pauline if she was alright.

She replied in a loud whisper. "I gotta pee."

BEHIND THE COUNTER, Dean leaned back, trying to figure his next move. In less than 24 hours, he had gone from being a disgruntled desk jockey to being caught in a shootout with the Russian mob. With several civilians caught in the crossfire.

Be careful what you wish for, he thought to himself.

To make matters worse, Jade had escaped. His whole reason for being here. At least he had got to see her. Sort of. Granted, he never got a great look at her face, but it was more than what anyone else had ever had to go on. Also, he got to see her in action. The impressive flip move she had made to break the standoff was exactly the type of ninja style attack Dean had imagined she would be capable of. He'd never admit it to any of his fellow agents, but Dean had been more than a little starstruck. But he couldn't be thinking about any of that right now. He had Russian fish to fry.

Dean turned to Randy.

"This your store?" he asked.

"It's my brother's. Well, technically it's my mama's."

Dean stopped him.

"You have any other guns? Under the register? In the back?"

Randy shook his head.

"There's a shotgun," Mama whispered.

Dean and Randy both looked at the woman.

"Clyde hid it in back," she explained. "It was his 'just-in-case gun'. It's in the old guitar case."

"Where is that?" Dean asked.

"It's behind the Bell Jar boxes," Mama explained. "On top of the bin where he keeps the old deer horns."

Dean nodded. "Okay. I'll be right back."

Randy shook his head.

"No. I'll go."

"Don't you go do nothing stupid," Mama whispered. "Let the law handle this."

"He ain't gonna be able to find it," Randy said. "They need my help. I'll be okay."

Mama smiled proudly. "You're a good boy, Randall."

"You stay put," he said. "I couldn't live with myself if anything happened to you."

He looked at Dean and used complicated hand motions to explain where he was going. Dean nodded, only half understanding the bizarre gesticulations. Randy then turned to his mother and smiled before crawling toward the backroom doorway.

62

"Has everyone caught their breath?" Viktor yelled out sarcastically.

The sheriff was the first to reply.

"Backup is on its way," he yelled. "Turn over your weapons now and this doesn't have to go bad."

"I want Jade," Viktor replied. "And I want my diamond."

"Can someone tell me who the holy hell Jade is?" Mama yelled.

The sheriff caught Dean's eye and motioned that he was going to crawl around the far side of the store to sneak up on the Russians. Understanding the sheriff's gestures, Dean motioned for him to wait, pointing out that he could more easily do it from his vantage point. He pointed to the front door, signaling for the sheriff to keep it covered. Now all Dean needed to do was keep the Russian mob boss occupied for a minute. He spoke to Mama loud enough for everyone to hear.

"Jade is a jewel thief and assassin for hire who is wanted by the FBI."

"Jade stole my diamond and killed my brother," Viktor corrected.

"Who. Is. Jade?" Mama repeated.

"Covering for her will only make things worse," Viktor said.

Finally, Mama put two and two together.

"Lord all Mighty," she said to no one in particular. "Our Jen is your Jade?"

"I knew she was trouble from the get-go!" Stonewall yelled.

Dean began to crawl around the perimeter of the store.

"Mister, I don't know Jade or Jen or Whatever Her Name Is did to you, but none of us know nothing about any of that," Mama said. "We are innocent."

"Because of you, she has escaped with my diamond," Viktor snapped.

"I don't know nothing about diamonds, mister," Mama said. "But that weren't even that big."

Viktor smirked.

"That diamond was part of the collection of the Romanov Dynasty," he explained. "It was priceless. And now it is gone because of...."

Before he could finish his sentence, Randy emerged from the backroom with a shotgun pointed directly at Viktor.

"You leave my mama alone, you son of a bitch," he demanded.

Leo aimed his gun at Randy but was quicky decommissioned by the butt of Dean's pistol. He dropped, unconscious, and Dean, who had successfully snuck up behind the Russians, turned his gun on Viktor.

"You heard the man," he said.

Viktor smiled at Dean and then turned to Randy.

"I don't think you want to do that," he said.

"Oh, believe me," Randy countered. "I really, really do."

"But what about your mother?" Viktor asked.

Randy turned to see Peter standing behind his mother, one hand over her mouth and the other holding a gun to her head.

63

N ow that Viktor and his goons had Mama as their hostage, they were able to quickly get everyone else to lay down their weapons. Finding some rope in the back room, they tied everyone up and sat them in a line along the front wall. Viktor forced the sheriff to call off the reinforcements, saying it was a false alarm, and threatened to shoot everyone if he even suspected seeing law enforcement.

Feeling in control again, Viktor paced back and forth in front of his captive audience, stopping in front of Dean.

"Do you know where she went?" he asked.

"Of course not," Dean answered.

Viktor nodded and paced some more, finally stopping in front of Randy. He crouched down in front of him.

"But you do," he said.

Randy shook his head.

"I don't even know who she is," he protested.

"But you both run after this one," Viktor said, pointing to a still-unconscious Amy Jo, who was propped up and tied at the end of the row.

"I was running after Jen, or Jade, to stop her from doing anything drastic," Randy said.

"Are you to meet later?" Viktor asked. "Do you think she will show?"

"We thought she was from Dallas," Mama interjected.

Viktor nodded at Mama and smiled.

"A high-faluttin' big city girl?" he teased, faking a Southern accent on top of his Russian accent.

He turned his attention back to Randy.

"I am curious," he said. "Did you think you had chance with her? You think she would, how you say, sink that low?"

Randy hung his head, embarrassed and ashamed in front of everyone.

"It wasn't like that," he muttered.

Viktor lifted his chin with the barrel of his gun.

"But you wished it."

"If anyone was sinking it was Randy," Mama snapped. "He's better than her and he's better than you."

Viktor smiled at Mama, unthreatened by her words. He turned his attention back to Dean.

"We take FBI man's car," he said. "And, couple of hostages."

He stood and walked back and forth, considering each potential candidate.

"Of course, you," he said, pointing at Dean. "FBI is protective of their own. But woman would also be nice."

He looked at Mama, then Pauline, then Amy Jo. He pointed at Amy Jo and addressed Mama.

"You call her tramp, da?"

Mama nodded and Viktor smiled.

"You can tell," he said with a wink.

Mama looked around at everyone with an 'I-told-you-so' look.

"Does she have children?" Viktor asked.

When Mama replied that she didn't, he shook his head.

"She will not do then," he said. "Even with heart of gold."

He looked Pauline up and down.

"And this one," he said. "On plus side, she would not take up much room."

"I still gotta pee," Pauline protested.

"Moving on," Viktor said, walking in front of Mama and kneeling down. "The Thunder Woman. Mama. May I call you Mama?"

"You most certainly may not," Mama said.

Viktor slapped her. Not hard, but hard enough for her to know he wasn't playing.

"You are wrong. I call you whatever the hell I want."

He stood again.

"But I have feeling you would not be worth grief you will most certainly cause," he said. "Maybe FBI agent is enough."

He walked over to Dean and demanded the keys to his rental car then turned to Peter and Leo.

"Keep agent. Kill others."

He turned to leave but froze in his tracks when he found himself staring directly in the face of Jade.

64

J ade smiled at a stunned Viktor.

"Sorry," she said. "You know how I hate to leave a mess."

Before he could respond, she leveled him with a power kick to the chest that sent him sailing into a shelf. Leo and Peter both turned and raised their guns but were no match for Jade's lightning-fast moves.

Flip. Punch. Kick. Spin.

In a flurry of motion, she kicked both guns out of the Russians' hands and threw Leo into the wall. He toppled to the ground like a ragdoll. Peter pulled a knife and lunged at her, but she dodged his attack, leaning to the side and using his own momentum to flip him to the floor, grabbing the knife in the process.

She rushed to Randy, cutting his binds and handing him the knife.

"Free the others and get out," she said before turning her attention back to the Russians.

All three of them had struggled back to their feet and charged Jade. She fended each of them off in a blur of kicks and punches. When Randy freed Dean, the agent rushed to assist Jade. Randy helped Mama to her feet and tried to guide her outside, but she shook off his arm.

"Oh, hell no," she said, storming toward the action.

Jade punched Peter and he spun around, where he was met with another powerful nose punch from Mama. The henchman dropped to his knees and Pauline, who had charged into the chaos, reared back a foot and kicked him hard between the legs. Several times.

As Stonewall and Toby slid along the back wall, avoiding the fight, Pauline continued her attack, maniacally throwing goat figurines at the Russians. Unfortunately, her aim wasn't that good, and she accidentally pelted Sheriff McKinney in the back of the head. He fell to the ground unconscious, his face landing in Amy Jo's lap.

After trading several punches with Leo, Dean soon lost the upper hand and found himself pinned against the wall. Leo began to choke him and Dean struggled to breath. He stared into the Russian's menacing eyes and saw them suddenly grow wide in surprise. His grip released from Dean's throat and he fell to the ground. Jade had come up from behind him and hit him over the head with a large terracotta goat head. Dean nodded in appreciation at his unlikely battle partner and Jade nodded back in acknowledgement.

Mama spotted Peter's pistol lying on the floor on the other side of the room. With the moves of a college fullback, she plowed toward it, dodging and weaving and pushing people out of her way. She scooped up the gun and made her way through the chaos to Viktor, grabbing him and firing the gun into the air.

Everyone froze and turned to see Mama holding the pistol to Viktor's temple.

"You better get to your knees, boys," she shouted. "And start praying to God I calm the hell down real quick."

Viktor raised his hands in surrender and slowly dropped to his knees. Peter and Leo followed suit. Dean pulled out his cuffs and put Viktor's hands behind his back while Randy gently took the gun from his mother's hands. Knowing things were under control, Stonewall picked up the other stray gun and held it on Leo and Peter.

"I got these two goons for ya," he announced heroically.

Randy surveyed the room to make sure everyone was accounted for. Coming up one short, he looked outside toward his truck.

65

J ade crouched in Randy's truck, trying to spark two wires and jumpstart the engine.

"Hey!"

"Shit," Jade muttered upon hearing Randy's voice.

She worked more frantically to hotwire the truck, but Randy opened the truck door before she could get a spark.

"Get out of my way, Randy," she said.

"Maybe these will help," Randy said.

Jade looked up to see Randy's truck keys dangling in front of her. She sat up, shocked, and took them from him.

"I promise I'll take good care of her," she said. "I'll leave her at the border. Unharmed. At least by me."

She started the engine.

"Thanks for coming back," Randy said.

Jade smiled.

"What? And miss all the fun?" she teased. "Besides, I was afraid of what your mother might do to them."

"I'm never gonna forget you," Randy said.

Jade smiled. "You might."

On a whim, she leaned forward and kissed him on the

cheek. Then, in what would easily be the bravest thing Randy had done in a day filled with heroics, he took her head in his hands and kissed her back on the lips. He meant for it to be a short, gentle kiss, but they found themselves pulling toward each other and kissing harder. Finally, she pulled away and grinned.

"Well, now you certainly won't," she said.

An ear-to-ear grin spread over Randy's face and Jade laughed as she shut the truck door.

"Take care of yourself, Randy," she said through the open window. "Remember, no one else is gonna do it for you."

And with that parting shot, she peeled away, leaving a cloud of red clay dust in her wake.

Dean rushed out of The Lazy Goat and, seeing Jade speed away, fumbled for his cell phone. But before he could dial a number, Mama walked up behind him and grabbed the phone out of his hands.

"What the hell do you think you're doing?" she demanded.

"She's getting away!" Dean protested.

"Exactly," Mama replied with a smile.

Dean watched helplessly as the truck drove out of sight. He looked at Mama and then at Randy, finally nodding in surrender. But as he put his phone away, he smiled.

"Good luck," he muttered under his breath.

Then he turned to the mother and son.

"But she only got away because I let her," he said with a wink.

66

Randy pulled on a fresh T-shirt. It had been one helluva day. It wasn't long after Jade left that a drove of police, FBI, paramedics and media vans took over the parking lot. The rest of the day had been spent in interrogations and interviews. Lucas had collected Clyde's body and moved the funeral out a day. This time it would be a small family affair. Mama's orders.

He turned when he heard a soft knock at his door to see his mother.

"Mind if I come in?" she said in an uncharacteristically soft voice.

She sat down on the edge of Randy's bed.

"Well, ain't this been a day for the record books?" she joked.

"How are you?" Randy asked. "You feeling alright?"

Mama waved him off. "I'm fine. Ain't nothing your mama can't handle."

Randy laughed and Mama reached out and grabbed his hands.

"Randall, I know I can be a truckload sometimes. And you may think I always favored your brother. But you need to know

I showed him more love because I knew he couldn't make it on his own. I never worried about that with you. But maybe sometimes I forgot you needed your Mama, too."

Randy sat down beside her, not knowing what to say.

"You were the golden child. The one that could do whatever he wanted. You still can."

Randy shook his head. "I can't complain, Mama."

"No, because that ain't your nature. But your dreams are too big for this little town, son. And I sure as hell ain't gonna stand in your way if you wanna go catch big fish in Florida."

Randy was stunned. Before he could even ask how she knew, Mama answered.

"A mama always knows," Mama said, fudging the truth a little bit. "Now I need you to help me bury your brother and sell the Lazy Goat, but you call your friend and tell him you're coming. I always wanted to visit Florida anyway."

"Are you sure?"

"Have I ever said anything I didn't mean?"

Randy laughed and gave her a big hug.

"I love you, Mama."

"You sure as hell better. I saved your ass today."

"You two get in here!" Pauline yelled from the other room. "It's starting!"

The mother and son walked into the living room just as the news report started.

A female reporter stood in The Lazy Goat parking lot that was swarming with FBI trucks, police cars, ambulances and news vans.

"Earlier today, the sleepy little East Texas town of Red Dirt became the scene of a violent hostage situation that has resulted in the apprehension of several suspects, including the alleged head of a notorious Russian crime family."

"This is it!" Pauline yelled.

Mama shushed her sister with a wave of her hand as the reporter continued.

"One of the hostages was Lucille Philpot, known to locals as Mama. Lucille, can you tell us what happened?"

The camera pulled back to reveal Mama standing proudly next to the reporter. Pauline was standing next to Mama but was cut out of frame except for when she occasionally leaned her head in to smile at the camera.

"I watch you all the time on TV," Mama said to the reporter. "You wear a lot more makeup in person. And you're a skinny little thang."

The reporter nodded graciously and repeated her question to Mama.

"I was fixing to get to it. Calm down," Mama said. "We was at my son Clyde's funeral. Rest his sweet soul."

She went on to describe how '*the stripper skank had caused all sorts of problems.*' How her son was the big hero of the day and how the sheriff had taken a bullet protecting her sister. No mention was made of Jade. When pushed for more information, Mama stated, in a very offical-sounding voice, that '*the event was under investigation and she wasn't allowed to say anything else.*'

Mama beamed at her television debut.

"You looked real nice, Lucy," Pauline said.

"I couldn't be prouder," Randy said, his arm wrapped tight around his mother's shoulder.

67

One week later...

Giant pieces of plywood covered the broken windows of the building formerly known as The Lazy Goat. The iconic sign near the road had been removed and construction equipment littered the empty parking lot.

Stonewall's truck sputtered past a cement mixer and parked in front of the building. He and Toby stepped out and surveyed the situation.

"I see you're putting that insurance money to good use," Stonewall sneered loudly for anyone to hear. "I sure hope you set some of it aside."

When no one answered, he decided to go inside to make sure his threat was heard. But the doorknob was locked.

"Don't think you can hide in there," Stonewall yelled.

"Oh, that door's locked," a voice said matter-of-factly.

Stonewall and Toby turned to see Dean walking around from the rear of the store. Dressed in a a filthy T-shirt and jeans, and wearing safety glasses and work gloves, he was almost unrecognizable.

"Not quite ready for business yet," he said with a smile.

"Where's Randy?" Stonewall stammered, unable to hide his surprise.

Dean shrugged and laughed.

"Who knows with that kid, right?"

He took his work gloves off.

"Anything I can do for you boys?"

"What are you doing here?" Toby asked.

"Getting my place ready," Dean said proudly.

He told his two visitors how he had fallen in love with the area and decided to stay. He bought The Lazy Goat and was converting it into his passion project. He turned to look at the building, imagining the sign out front.

"The Burrito Palace and Goat Emporium."

He turned back around to the two confused faces.

"Part of the deal was I still need to sell goat figurines," he explained. "That Mama can be a hard bargainer."

"This is bullshit," Stonewall growled.

"I know. I know," Dean said. "Why compete with Perty's? But it was their idea. They're my partners. They get to expand, and I get a fresh start."

"What kind of burritos?" Toby asked.

"All kinds," Dean answered. "And fresh made. Local."

"Randy owes us money," Stonewall griped. "So by proxy, you owe us money."

Dean raised a finger and pulled a set of keys from his pocket. He unlocked the front door and walked inside. Stonewall and Toby tried to peak in, but Dean walked back out before they had a chance.

"Nuh-uh. It's gotta be a surprise," he said.

He handed a thick manilla envelope to Stonewall.

"That's from Randy. He figured you'd be stopping by. It's everything he owes you."

Stonewall looked in the envelope.

"It's all there," Dean said. "Plus the $200 interest."

"I'll count it later," Stonewall said, handing the envelope to Toby.

"If you don't mind," Dean said. "I've got a lot of work to do."

He turned his back on the two men, locked the front door and started walking around back.

"Your gonna need some protection for your new place here," Stonewall yelled out to him.

Dean waved his hand, never turning around.

"I'm good," he replied.

Stonewall's voice grew deep and threatening. "I weren't making a suggestion."

Dean turned around and squinted at the tall man and his odd-looking companion.

"Are you threatening a federal agent?" Dean asked. "I'm still with the bureau, Stonewall. I'm just on vacation right now. I got three months to go before I can retire early. So you best watch what you say. And what you do. The FBI does not take kindly to threats of any kind. Even to former agents. You understand?"

"Oh. And while I'm gone, my good friend Sheriff McKinley is going to be keeping an eye on things. If anything happens, he's coming straight for you."

He smiled and waved.

"I'll be back before you know it. And just so you know there's no hard feelings, when we open, your first burrito is on me."

Stonewall and Toby watched Dean walk around the back of the building.

"Free burrito," Toby said quietly. "That ain't so bad."

68

Three months later...

The raucous group of fishermen walked into the open-air Florida bar situated on the far edge of the harbor. It was nothing fancy, nothing like the tourist bars on the other side of the harbor. This was the drinking place for the locals and the harbor workers. It's also where Randy liked to bring his charter customers after a day of deep sea fishing. They enjoyed the "authentic" experience and the bar got a little extra money.

Today, Randy brought in a group of six. Four businessmen on vacation. Two of them brought their teenage sons. Randy always bought the first round so, after making sure everyone had a drink, he walked to the bar to settle up. As he waited to pay, a woman sat down next to him. She wore large aviator sunglasses and a baseball hat pulled down low.

"Sea life suits you, sailor," she said.

Randy instantly recognized her voice. He turned to Jade as she removed her glasses and smiled. He barely recognized her. She had short black hair and wore minimal makeup. But there was no mistaking her eyes and he couldn't help but think she was more beautiful than ever.

"Jen? I mean, Jade? I mean…"

He opened his arms to hug her but held back, not knowing what he should do. Jade laughed and extended her own arms, letting him know it was okay. The hug was sincere but still very awkward.

"What are you doing here?" Randy asked.

"Can't a lady check in on her ex-boyfriend?" she asked with a wink.

"How did you find me?"

Jade laughed. "Have you forgotten who I am?"

Randy sat down and bought them both a drink. He caught her up on everything. How Mama had sent him on his way, but only with the promise to visit once a month. She laughed hard when he told her he had sold the Lazy Goat to the FBI agent. He asked her what she had been up to and, even though she never stopped smiling, she grew quiet and shrugged.

"I'm getting out of the business," she said. "I've put enough away and that last job paid pretty good."

"So what are you gonna do now?" Randy asked.

"Do I have to do anything?" she asked. "I'm just going to enjoy life for a bit. See what happens."

"If you ever wanna go deep-sea fishing, I know a guy."

Jade smiled. Randy noticed how much more relaxed she seemed.

"I mean, I'm sure you've got a lot more exciting and luxurious things to do than that," he said.

"No," she replied. "I'd like that. Very much."

She stood, explaining she needed to get going. There was still some outstanding business she needed to take care of, but she promised to call. They hugged awkwardly again, and she started to leave only to stop and turn back around.

"Valerie," she said.

"I'm sorry?" Randy asked, confused.

"My real name is Valerie."

Randy smiled. "Nice to meet you, Valerie."

"I'll see you soon," she said with a smile and a wink.

She squeezed Randy's hand gently and then quietly walked away.

~

THE END

THANK YOU FOR READING
RED DIRT BLUES

If you enjoyed it, be sure to leave a review wherever you bought your copy. A review can go a long way in helping other readers find this book.

GET YOUR FREE COPY OF *BOUND BY MURDER*
This fun and riveting mystery novella e-book is available for free at **davidkwilsonauthor.com**

ALSO BY DAVID K. WILSON:

COMBUSTIBLE - SAM LAWSON MYSTERY 1

When Texas detective Sam Lawson stumbles upon the dark side of a victim's past, he is soon caught in a maze of murder, abuse and corruption.

BENEATH THE SURFACE - SAM LAWSON MYSTERY 2

Everyone's favorite hard-living detective investigates the mysterious disappearance of a young woman and discovers everyone has something to hide.

DARK HARBOR - SAM LAWSON MYSTERY 3

This suspenseful page-turner follows Sam on vacation to Martha's Vineyard where he gets caught up in a brutal murder investigation.

Learn more at davidkwilsonauthor.com

ACKNOWLEDGMENTS

A big thank you goes out to Shelley Upchurch, who not only offered a ton of invaluable suggestions during the writing of this book but also gave me much-needed support and encouragement when I needed it most.

I also want to thank Julia Zave for keeping my Russian references as legit as possible, Cyndi Stripling for her mad proofreading skills and Caroline Johnson for hitting another cover design out of the park. And a big shout-out goes to a group of super humans who also happen to be fellow authors: Lorraine Evanoff, Yvonne Pelletier, James Hewitson and Barbara Fournier. Your advice and feedback always make me a better writer.

Last but not least, I want to thank my extended family who always have my back, and whose stories—both real and fabricated—inspired many of the adventures in this book.

ABOUT THE AUTHOR

David K. Wilson grew up in East Texas, surrounded by enough colorful characters to fill the pages of hundreds of books. Author of the popular Sam Lawson Mystery series, David is also a seasoned ghostwriter, screenwriter and songwriter. He currently lives in upstate New York, where he still complains about winter every single year.

Sign up to receive updates on David's next novel at davidkwilsonauthor.com.